MURDER
IN THE
STABLEYARD

An addictive crime mystery full of twists

ROY LEWIS

Arnold Landon Mysteries Book 4

Originally published as
Men of Subtle Craft

D1493646

BOOKS

Revised edition 2021
Joffe Books, London
www.joffebooks.com

First published in Great Britain in 1987
as *Men of Subtle Craft*

ISBN: 978-1-78931-847-0

NOTE TO THE READER

Please note this book is set in the 1980s in England,
a time before mobile phones and ubiquitous CCTV,
and when social attitudes were very different.

CHAPTER ONE

1

The twig cracked, with a light snapping sound. The doe's head came up sharply, her body tense, muscles ready to surge into action.

The eyes made out nothing to cause the animal further alarm. She was unable to distinguish the form of the hunter in the trees: the camouflaged shirt and stained jeans enabled the motionless figure to merge into the background. Wind direction had been gauged, woollen socks had been pulled over stout leather boots to muffle the sound underfoot, and there had been only the mishap of the broken twig to raise the alarm.

In a little while the doe, satisfied, resumed feeding, her hide dappled by the early evening sun that filtered low through the trees and cast long shadows down towards the stream fifty feet below. It was towards the burn that the deer made their way as dusk fell.

Across the stream the hill rose, open farmland stretching away beyond the deer fence to the hazy, craggy outlines of Cheviot. A blue haze of smoke rose lazily in the air from a distant wood fire and the road that crossed the bridge over the stream was empty, a dusty track winding its way over the ridge to the lonely farm on the hill.

The hunter paid no attention to the view across the stream. The arrow slid gently from its quiver and was now set, nock against bowstring.

This arrow was utterly unlike the mediaeval clothyard shafts that had been used on ancient battlefields. It was a fine-tuned missile of drawn aluminium, made in the United States. There were no grey goose feathers in the fletching of the tubular shaft, instead flexible waterproof nylon vanes gave it an almost silent accuracy.

The doe's head was down, snuffling, as the bow slowly came up.

Aerospace technology had spawned this weapon: this was no traditional longbow of solid yew or hickory. The cam bow was a sinister-looking contraption with a diecast magnesium alloy handle and polished limbs of laminated graphite and epoxy resins. Cables and aluminium cams took the strain until the bow was fully drawn, and the arrow, with its multi-bladed broad head of shatterproof stainless steel was designed to be released at an explosive speed of one hundred and ninety feet per second, its razor-sharp cutting edges capable of slicing through the toughest hide like butter.

At the last second the doe raised her head. Perhaps it was some instinctive feeling that presaged danger; perhaps she had heard the slight hiss of breath from the hunter as the full draw-weight of the bow was taken. The animal stared straight at the hunter, poised for flight, but it was too late. The arrow sang, there was a blur of light, a flash as the sun caught the flight of the missile, and then the doe was gone, collapsing sideways as the arrow thudded home behind the shoulder.

The hunter was aware that it was virtually impossible to kill cleanly with one flight. The thrashing of the animal in the undergrowth was noisy, mixed with a coughing sound as the doe spat streams of blood and kicked, trying to rise against the missile that had half paralysed her.

She was still kicking when the hunter finally stood above her, staring down dispassionately. The first arrow had broken a rib, sliced through the lung, lodged in the spleen. The doe was still quivering after the second arrow slashed through the belly and pierced the liver, but the eyes were glazing coldly.

The hunter was breathing lightly, but quickly, as though excited by the thrashing and the blood. But like the animal just killed, the hunter's senses were also keen, sharpened to the environment and the intimation of danger.

There was someone nearby.

Bowhunting in England was an illegal activity. Local magistrates could be hard on offenders, particularly up here in the Cheviots. The hunter remained still for several seconds, then moved smoothly and quietly through the ferns beneath the trees to a vantage-point, screened by pines, above the road.

The man standing on the track below seemed to have emerged from nowhere. He was stockily built and wore a tweed jacket with patched elbows, hands thrust in his pockets. He had taken off his hat, and the early evening sun gleamed on the scalp that showed through his thinning hair. He was standing, feet braced apart, staring up the slope directly towards the spot where the deer had died, moments ago.

The hunter glanced around carefully. The man below was alone. It was likely he had come down from the farm on the hill, or had walked up along the burn, below the fold of the ridge where he would have been invisible to anyone in the trees, until he reached the track where he now stood, glaring suspiciously in the direction of the hunter.

The man hesitated, half turned to walk away along the track and then stopped again, swinging his head to scan the treeline. His face was tanned, his eyebrows heavy and black, a contrast to his thinning hair, and the hunter recognized him, knew him.

He was a man who deserved to die.

It would be a long shot, but not a difficult one. The man standing on the track would never know what had hit him. That would be a pity . . . and it would be a pity he would never know who had released the arrow in his direction.

With studied care the hunter in the trees slid an arrow out of the quiver. The broad head was fine-edged under a questing thumb. It would be capable, at this distance, of punching a hole four inches square in the target on the roadway.

The hunter nocked the arrow, raised the bow and the first pull raised the sophisticated sights with their calibrated tracks until the hunter could pick out the lapels of the tweed jacket. The sights moved fractionally; the centre of the man's chest was targeted and the cables and aluminium cams began to take the strain as the hunter drew smoothly, left arm rigid against the cable guard, gloved right hand holding the tense bowstring.

An expelling of breath, a light, long drawing in of air, a holding, a savouring of the moment before the deadly broadhead would skim through the air on its lethal mission . . .

A coughing sound broke the silence of the hillside, a rumbling noise, an approaching car from the right where the road swung around past the screening trees. The hunter froze, instinct calling for a release of the bowstring, inclination urging the destruction of the man in the roadway, but an innate caution holding back the action, calling for control. If the car came around the bend, and the man was lying stricken in the roadway . . .

It was a small Ford, silver-grey in colour, and it came rumbling around the hill, slowing as the driver caught sight of the man in the roadway. The hunter could make out the driver as a woman, and it was obvious the opportunity was gone unless two people were to die on the evening hillside. The gloved hand lost some of its tension as the hunter breathed out again. The cables smoothly took up the relaxing strain and the aluminium speed cams whirred silently to rest.

The car had slowed, was stopping, and the woman behind the wheel was leaning out to call to the man in the roadway. The words were indistinguishable, but clearly the driver had come out to meet the man in the roadway, bring him back from his evening walk. After a short discussion the man, somewhat bad-temperedly, got into the car. The woman found it difficult to reverse the vehicle and a stream of blue exhaust stained the air before she managed to swing the car around on the narrow track and head it back the way she had come.

The hunter was silent on the hill, shadowed completely by the trees, watching, with an ache of disappointment. The crags that rose to Cheviot were purpling now, and the sky above was darkening from its pale blue to a deeper hue. From the distant farm there was the sound of a dog barking, and as the car vanished around the bend the sound of its engine rapidly faded.

A soft silence returned to the hill. There was no movement from the doe now, but her death seemed to have affected the woods. There was no birdsong, no movement in the undergrowth, and the Cheviot itself seemed stricken, waiting for danger to pass and death to reach out to nothing else on the hill.

The hunter replaced the arrow in the quiver. There were two more arrows to recover from the still warm, quivering body of the deer. They would be cleaned in the grass as darkness gathered under the trees, and then the body of the dead beast would have to be dragged down the hill to the car hidden in the dry gully some three hundred yards away. The exercise was not to be relished: it was an anti-climax after the smooth, quiet efficiency of the stalking and the kill.

Therein lay the excitement: the long waiting when nothing seemed about to happen; the quick heartbeat at the first signs, the first sounds of movement in the undergrowth; then the stalking, silent under the trees until the pent-up, heart-stopping tension in those seconds before the arrow exploded into flight.

That moment was almost orgasmic. Now, there remained only a vague irritation at the thought of hauling the carcase down to the car.

But this day there had been that other moment to savour, a moment that could be weighed and enjoyed for its tension, its bunching of hate and muscle, commitment and excitement. The bow sight had been concentrated on the centre of the target's chest and the hunter could still envision the blood-soaked image that had been relayed: a hole punched in a man's chest, life blood pulsing out to stain the ground as sightless eyes stared skywards.

Not the eyes of a doe; the eyes of a man.

The hunter stared down the empty road. It had been close. Seconds . . . a second, and the act would have been done. If the woman in the silver-grey Ford had not appeared to call away her employer it would have happened, it would have been done. As it *needed* to be done. The man down there deserved to die.

The hunter smiled reflectively.

He deserved to die, and it could be done. But this would not necessarily be the only opportunity.

There would be another time: perhaps soon.

But now, there was the deer. The hunter moved, to retrieve the arrows, and then stopped, hair rising at the nape of the neck. Some thirty yards away, crouched against a tussock of grass, was a dog. It was lean, alert and watchful, its body tensed as though ready to spring and the hunter stared at it as the low rumbling came from the animal's throat.

The adrenalin began to pump again in the hunter's veins. Thirty yards: swift mental calculations, and the dog crouched lower, belly against the ground, its sheepdog frame quivering as it bared its teeth at the smell of blood, and the threat it sensed as the hunter's tension was communicated to it. Its eyes glistened as the hunter's hand moved slowly towards the quiver, and it heard the smooth hiss of the arrow sliding from its home.

The hunter moved slowly, precisely, eyes fixed on those of the dog, hands and arms moving gently, engaging the nock, raising the bow until the arrowhead rose, its needle point lining up with the black and white shoulder of the dog. The animal rose slightly, the rumbling threatening in its throat and the hunter breathed in, gently, waiting for the moment.

The twig cracked loudly, snapping like a dry bone in the silence of the woods. The arrowhead dropped, wavering as the hunter glanced around, quickly and nervously. When the rustling came from among the trees it was followed by movement, a dark frame thrusting its way through the undergrowth behind the dog.

The hunter lowered the bow as the tall man came walking down the hillside, snapping his fingers to the dog. It responded, hackles lowering immediately, even though it kept its eyes fixed on the threat of the longbow.

The man was lean. He moved with a long, patient stride that showed he walked these hills regularly, and his tanned skin made it obvious that he spent much time in the open. His dark jacket was elderly and patched at cuffs and elbows and his battered hat was pulled low across his forehead, pinning the thick grey hair into place.

He reached the dog and stood there for several seconds, staring at the hunter with the lowered bow. He creased his eyes, and his glance was sharp, weighing up the situation, aware of the tension, and something angry danced in those eyes as he stared at the hunter, anger and disgust mixed in a shadow of dislike.

Then the glance slipped away, almost inadvertently, to take in the silent road below, before returning to the dog, and the bow, and the hunter. It was then that the hunter knew that this man had seen all that had occurred — the death of the deer, the arrival of the man in the road below, the moment when that arrow had almost been loosened. There was one, slow moment when fear prickled against the hunter's skin, and then it was gone.

The man with the dog had his own reasons to hate. If the arrow *had* exploded towards its mark he might even have melted away over the hill. He would have his own reasons to want the man in the roadway dead, and he would not interfere with the hunter now.

The dog rose, to nuzzle against the owner's leg. The hunter moved too, sneeringly, replacing the arrow in the quiver, moving to pick up the other shafts.

When they had been cleaned in the long grass the hunter looked up. The man with the dog had gone.

2

In the courtyard in front of the Newcastle University History Faculty building two young students sat with their backs to the wall and their arms around each other. As he walked past them Arnold Landon felt vaguely uneasy. At moments like this he definitely felt his age. It was not that he objected to public expression of affection by the young — far from it. He considered the irreverence young people always showed for their elders to be a healthy sign, a signal that they would not accept the *mores* of a previous generation as gospel. At the same time he felt uneasy, for he was not exactly sure what the sex of either of the two lovers on the lawn might be. The permutations were, admittedly, limited in their possibilities, but some of them left him uneasy. And feeling his age.

He entered the wide doors, admiring the entrance hall, and approached the desk behind which the porter, corpulent in a slightly shabby uniform, sat reading a tabloid newspaper.

'Excuse me. I'd like to see Professor Evesham.'

'He expecting you, sir?'

'At ten.'

The porter inspected the clock on the wall behind him. It was just two minutes before the hour. He seemed pleased with such punctuality and smiled vaguely at Arnold, put down his newspaper and reached for the telephone.

As he called Professor Evesham's office Arnold looked about him. He had not entered these buildings before. The hallway had some interesting features. The archway leading to the offices on the right was built of stone of a light creamy-yellow colour. Clipsham stone, he guessed, although it might have been part of an old consignment of Caen stone that had found its way northward in the vogue for using such stone that had occurred in the 'thirties, when much of the present university building had taken place. Odd, that; a thirteenth-century fad for Caen stone being repeated in the nineteen-thirties. Not least when there was perfectly good local stone that looked much the same available from Beer or Clipsham.

'Mr Landon?' The porter dragged Arnold back to the present. 'Professor Evesham is able to see you in his room. It's straight up the stairs, around to the right through the swing doors, and third on the left.'

Arnold followed the directions given. He found himself in a narrow corridor, facing a half-open door labelled with a dog-eared card bearing the legend *Alan Evesham*. Arnold tapped on the door and it swung wide quickly, as though the occupant had been waiting behind it.

'Landon? Good. I'll be back in a minute.'

The man was gone before Arnold could reply. Arnold hesitated, then entered the room. It was a complete clutter. The table below the mullioned window was scattered with papers, some of a certain antiquity. Arnold wondered for their safety as a light breeze rustled through the open window, lifting them.

A cigarette smouldered in the ashtray and Arnold stubbed it out, self-consciously, fearing for the papers. He looked around: leaning against the wall was a mediaeval pike; on the floor behind the desk was a fourteenth-century crossbow with a butt inlaid with chased metal. The wastepaper bin had been used as a makeshift quiver with ugly-looking bolts stuffed into it.

One wall was dominated by an ornately scrolled oak bookcase. As Arnold admired the workmanship he noted that Evesham's interests seemed warlike: the bookcase was packed with volumes ranging from second World War tactics to an account of Agincourt, with French military manoeuvres, Crimean histories and the Mexican war of the 1840s thrown in for good measure.

'Military history.'

Professor Alan Evesham was closing the door behind him with his left foot. He held his arms out stiffly, carrying two cups of coffee. One of the paper cups was already stained by a dribble of spilled liquid. Arnold nodded towards the books.

'Quite a collection. Your hobby, or simply what you teach at the university?'

'Hobby, work, passion,' Alan Evesham replied and slipped past Arnold through the clutter of the room. He kicked aside a dull-metalled breastplate and swore under his breath. Arnold waited.

Evesham put down a paper cup on his desk, finding the only free corner, handed the other to Arnold, wiped his right hand on the seat of his jeans and then stuck it out in welcome. 'Alan Evesham.'

'I'm pleased to meet you,' Arnold said warily.

Alan Evesham was not the kind of man he had expected to meet. When he had received a phone call from the university, with a request that he find time to call in to see a history professor, he had had a mental image of grey, middle-aged sobriety. But Alan Evesham was hardly more than thirty years old, with a shock of sandy hair, and narrow, bad-tempered eyes that would swing in expression from glittering enthusiasm, Arnold guessed, to virulent annoyance. The mouth too was the kind that would express impatience in a man who would be given to hasty judgements and eternal dislikes. Few students would like him perhaps, though his professorial post suggested that the university authorities respected him for his knowledge and ability.

'I've heard about you,' Evesham said sharply, and tugged at the hairy sweater he affected as though he disliked hearing about anyone other than himself 'You're reckoned to be quite an authority in certain fields.'

'I wouldn't put it quite like that.'

Evesham slumped in the chair behind his desk. After a moment Arnold took the seat facing him, noting that Evesham had made no pretence to politeness.

'Gifted amateur, then, is that it?'

There was a thinly veiled belligerence in his tone that was not unfamiliar to Arnold. He was used to meeting a certain resistance whenever he was called upon for consultation with the academic world. His reputation of recent years had grown because of his love for wood and stone — and the understanding of the past that had grown out of this obsession. There had been occasions when he had confounded the experts: this had endeared him neither to the Establishment nor to his own Senior Planning Officer, who regarded such activity as vaguely open to suspicion.

'I'm not sure I care to classify myself in any way,' Arnold responded mildly. 'I'm a planning officer, employed by Northumberland—'

'But you claim to know a lot about mediaeval times.'

'Claim, no—'

'Professor Agnew suggested I should enlist your help.'

So that was it. Arnold stared soberly at Alan Evesham. The man had not shaved that morning and there was a fine ginger stubble of beard on his chin. He cared little for appearances, that was certain; what he did care about was being told by a respected senior professor in the university that he might usefully turn for help and advice to a humble planning officer with no academic background.

'Professor Agnew has probably over-estimated my abilities.'

'Quite likely. But Professor Agnew is responsible for the allocation of certain grants . . .' Evesham glowered, then reached for his paper cup and sipped his coffee. 'You've seen the books on my shelves. You'll have realized I'm a military historian. At present I'm conducting an inquiry into the Middle Ages. Twelfth century, in fact.'

'Interesting.'

'Very. Agnew reckons I could consult you with advantage.'

'About military history? I'm afraid that's not quite—'

'Not your scene?' Evesham's brow furrowed impatiently. 'So what *is* your . . . field?'

Arnold hesitated. 'I'm not sure I'd claim one. I have a certain . . . knowledge about the use of stone in the Middle Ages, and I have been successful in dating various structures from the joints used in the timber—'

'So what do you know about master masons in the twelfth century?'

Arnold blinked. 'It depends what you want to know. I mean, it's common enough knowledge that stone buildings in the Middle Ages were erected by professional workmen. There is a large number of accounts which demonstrate that the work they undertook was under the control of a chief, or master, mason. The actual mason in charge might change from time to time, naturally, during the course of the work—'

'Do you know the names of any of these master masons?' Evesham interrupted.

'Well, a large proportion of these chief masons have left their names only in single building accounts. On the other hand, some of them can be traced in a succession of jobs in different parts of the country—'

'Ahhh.'

'I beg your pardon?'

Evesham shook his head impatiently, but his eyes were less hostile than previously, and there was an edge of surprised satisfaction to his mouth. 'Go on.'

Deliberately, Arnold took a sip of his coffee. It was weak and milky and he disliked the taste of it. He also resented the fact that he seemed to be in a situation where he was being called upon to prove something to Professor Alan Evesham.

'I'm not sure how you want me to go on, or why. If you want to know about the old master masons, well, some of them obtained official positions, of course.'

'Would you regard them as architects?'

Arnold shrugged. 'Not exactly, not in the modern sense. But they were responsible for the design and details of the buildings upon which they worked—'

'And so should be regarded as the architects of the Middle Ages, surely,' Evesham said testily.

'If you say so.'

'And the *ingeniatores?*'

Arnold raised his eyebrows.

'The *engineers*,' Evesham sneered.

'I was aware—'

'One such engineer was employed by Bishop Hugh Pudsey at Norham Castle. He described him as *vir artificiosus . . . et prudens architectus.*' Evesham smiled. 'The good bishop thought of the engineer in question as a prudent *architect.*'

'But he was talking about Ailnoth,' Arnold said quietly. He had been unable to resist the temptation and the reaction was satisfying.

Evesham's head came up and his mouth dropped open. He put down his paper cup, and his hand strayed to his mouth as though to rearrange his surprise. His mean little eyes had widened too, and respect was creeping into them together with astonishment. *'Ailnoth*! How do *you* know about him?'

'You don't have to have a university pedigree to be interested in and read about architecture,' Arnold remonstrated mildly. Now he had made his point he could afford to be generous. 'I have read . . . a little about the builders in the Middle Ages. While I work from a knowledge and an understanding of wood and stone I've also found it necessary to read . . . the experts.'

Evesham frowned, as though he was not quite sure if he was being mocked. He shook his head. 'All right, so you've heard about Ailnoth. What do you know about him?'

Arnold took a deep breath, nettled again by Evesham's manner. 'Well, I suppose I know a fair bit about him, really. In 1157, I know, he was surveyor of the King's buildings at Westminster—'

'—and The Tower.'

'He was paid the not insubstantial sum of seven pence per day—'

'—an annual salary of £10. 12s. 11d.'

'He supervised the purchase of stone and lead for work at Windsor Castle—'

'—between 1167 and 1173—'

'And after the rebellion of 1174 he was in charge of the dismantling of Framlingham and Walton Castles.'

Evesham sniffed. 'He also supervised work at Westminster Abbey when the *frater* had been burned.'

'I didn't think this was going to be set as an examination, Professor Evesham, nor as a competition. I don't see what either of us is getting out of this conversation.' Arnold hesitated. 'Professor Agnew suggested we talk. You seem to be satisfying yourself as to my . . . credentials. I don't really have any. And I certainly don't see how I can help you in any way, as far as military history is concerned.'

Evesham bit his lip in thought. Several seconds passed in silence before he nodded, forcing out the words. 'I'm sorry.'

Arnold shrugged. 'That's all right.'

Evesham eyed him silently for a little while. 'You seem,' he said reluctantly, 'to know about master masons . . . and more importantly, about Ailnoth. But you've missed one obvious fact.'

'What's that?'

'How most of them really spent their time.'

'I don't understand,' Arnold said slowly.

Evesham glanced at the papers on his desk and scratched his nose thoughtfully. 'The mediaeval age was a great church and cathedral building time. But it was notable for something else as well. It was a time of war.'

'So?'

'My interest isn't in church building or the erection of cathedrals. So why am I interested in what you know about masons? The truth is, masons in those days didn't spend most of their time on religious buildings. Think about it: Wulfric at Carlisle in 1172, Maurice at Newcastle in 1174, Richard at Bowes and Walton — they weren't concerned with churches. They were building *castles*.'

'I understand that.'

'But what you don't seem to have grasped, Landon, is that military works were the *primary* concern of these architects, these engineers. They were mainly concerned with military engines, with mangonels, catapults, trebuchets and so on. It was their job to design the defences which would allow them to use the artillery they possessed themselves and resist the weapons brought up by the besiegers. Look at the records again: when the existing west wall of the lower bailey of Windsor Castle was built with its three towers in 1228, the *master trebucheter* was one of the two persons appointed to supervise the work.'

'It's a point of view — and a fact — that had not come to my attention,' Arnold said slowly.

'Hmmm.' Alan Evesham was silent again for a little while. 'I suppose I have to credit Professor Agnew with more sense than I have done,' he said grumpily. 'Just as you won't have appreciated the significance of military history in ancient building operations, so my obsession with military history hasn't left me with time or inclination to look at the purely *building* implications surrounding the facts I seek. And that's why it occurred to Agnew to throw the two of us together.'

Arnold hesitated. 'I can understand the logic of Professor Agnew's suggestion, even if I feel I probably have little to offer. But what's the purpose of the . . . collaboration?'

The word collaboration drew dark colours of protest in Evesham's eyes; he quelled them as he came to terms with the fact that even this discussion was a collaboration, in a sense. He shrugged unwillingly. 'I mentioned earlier that Agnew is in charge of certain research allocations in the faculty. I've been working on a theory for some years, and I believe I've got conclusions which are valid, but which require proof, a certain verification, before I can publish. I think Agnew is quite keen for me to publish . . . but he insists that money is short. Bloody cuts . . .' he added gloomily.

'But where do I come in?'

'I went to Agnew when I learned he was going to phase out the research support grant. I explained, and I *know* he's interested, but . . . well, to cut a long story short, he said he didn't have the money to support the research. I'd have to take short cuts. One of them, he suggested, would be to pass up the opportunity to undertake my own research. Instead, I should use skills and knowledge already available to us in the North. You.'

'Me?'

'You,' Evesham repeated, scowling. 'It's question of a marriage of minds. You might bring a certain objective understanding to the situation, to supplement what I've learned and what I believe to be the truth.'

'It's very flattering—'

'No doubt,' Evesham said brusquely. 'But time is short. We have a couple of weeks only before I'm committed to a Scandinavian conference. I have to pick your brains at speed.'

'I see. At least,' Arnold added cautiously, 'I *think* I see. You questioned me about chief masons—'

'But specifically I'm interested in Ailnoth.'

'Ahh.'

'How much more do you know about him?'

Arnold shook his head. 'Not a great deal. I've only really come across his work in Framlingham and seen some of his building accounts. I was . . . er . . . boasting a little, really.'

'A shot in the dark, is it?' Evesham said gloomily. 'Well, no matter. I've been able to trace the movements of Ailnoth the *ingeniator*. He certainly got around a bit.'

'It was a common experience for masons,' Arnold suggested. 'Prominent masters of the craft were often employed at various locations in the country as consultants, and

17

sometimes as architects to supply the design from which the work was carried out.'

'It certainly happened with our friend Ailnoth,' Evesham agreed. 'He was sent with one Martin Simon, a carpenter, to view the site for a new castle the King wanted to build in York and within two months he was back at Westminster, having taken in a job at Beverley on the way.'

'In my own observations I've been able to trace work which was started by a mason from Exeter being completed by one from Stafford,' Arnold interrupted. 'And the work itself is in Durham.'

'Quite,' Evesham said rather crossly. 'The point is, I've managed to trace Ailnoth's career fairly clearly until about 1181. There's a hint he might have been involved at Dover Castle in 1181-2, but it's not absolutely clear, and after that date he seems to have dropped out of sight completely. At least, that's what scholarship would have you believe.'

'You've found evidence to the contrary?'

Evesham leaned forward in his chair, pushed aside the half-empty paper cup and began to rummage in his papers. 'Yes, here's my note. There's a couple of documents I rooted out in Canterbury; they lead me to believe there was some sort of scandal. Maybe corrupt practices of some kind.'

'That was not particularly uncommon.'

'I believe it. Things haven't changed. Anyway, I came across this document. It's the evidence of the Master of Works:

'There was removal of timber, stone and lime. I know not where it went. The roofing of the church and the stonework suffer injury through lack of care. The outer pilasters which are also called botraces have for the most part perished for defect of covering . . .

'The thing is, the works in question were under the control of Ailnoth. And I think he was disgraced by the inquiry that went on. But he didn't just drop out of sight.'

'What did he do?' asked Arnold curiously.

'The next best thing. Turned his hand to other aspects of the trade. More lowly but still remunerative. I think he started doing repairs — maybe the ones at Baynard's Castle in 1183. He became a supplier of plaster, stones and tiles.'

'You've got evidence for this?'

'Sketchy,' Evesham admitted.

'So where do I come in?'

Evesham hesitated. 'I'm really only interested in Ailnoth as a military *ingeniator*. I've been studying military installations in the North, dating back to the twelfth century. And I have a feeling . . . a gut reaction, if you like. I think Ailnoth came north after his disgrace. I think he worked as a supplier of materials, but from time to time, when requested, he threw in his abilities as a mason and an *ingeniator* as part of the deal he struck. I'm sure I can trace the movements of a man called Ailnoth in the North after 1182 — as a *supplier*. But was it the same Ailnoth?'

'You want *me* to try to find out?'

'Agnew says you've got an eye. No academic background, but an eye. And luck.'

Arnold wasn't sure whether he should feel pleased or slighted. 'I don't even know what you want me to look for.'

'You've heard of the disputes regarding Langton Castle?'

Arnold had been vaguely aware of academic discussions regarding the ruined castle north of Morpeth; they had been reported skimpily in the popular press.

'It's the ruins near Langton village in Northumberland. A thirteenth-century castle which was laid waste by the border raiders in the fifteenth century and was never rebuilt.'

'Thirteenth century, but with some walls possibly dating to the tenth.'

'In the tenth century buildings were made of timber.'

'But some stone.'

'Occasionally.'

'And maybe at Langton.'

'It's possible. But what do you want me to do? Inspect Langton Castle? I don't think I can do much—'

'I've already inspected it. As a military historian. I'd like you to look, from a building point of view. But first, I'd like you to meet me at the village itself. Or more precisely, at its church.'

'Why?'

'To show you what I think is the last resting-place of Ailnoth the *ingeniator*.'

* * *

As far as Arnold could make out it was a pretty thin thesis — and one not particularly important anyway. Alan Evesham was obsessed with the idea that the military architect he saw in Ailnoth had returned to the North after his work on the great castles, and in relative obscurity had continued his work, exercising his skills in Northumberland. But he had to admit he had no hard evidence of the work, although he was told by the vicar of the tiny church at Langton that the parish records contained some reference to the supplier of plaster and stone that Evesham sought. That the military historian was urgent in his need to discover the evidence to support the thesis was clear to Arnold: the Professor would never have turned to a 'gifted amateur' in other circumstances. But Arnold still doubted whether he truly had anything to offer.

The Senior Planning Officer was of like opinion.

Not that he was prepared to say so directly to Arnold. His predecessor had left the planning department under a cloud, and the new Senior Planning Officer seemed to feel that he had a cautious path to tread, one mined by subordinates who were disloyal, incompetent and unreliable. His solution to the problem had been to interview each of them in turn upon his arrival, make snap judgements, and then retire into the safety of his office, emerging rarely, and issuing instructions from time to time. They were usually succinct, to avoid misunderstanding, and precise to avoid responsibility.

Arnold had had his interview with the new Senior Planning Officer and he had been left in no doubt that his interests were regarded as bizarre and his experiences unsettling. He was to keep his personal activities clearly separate from his work for the department.

He had had his interview, and now he received his instructions.

'Report to Mr Sanders. University activity only in spare time. Relieve Mr Sanders of Kilgour House file.'

It did not take Arnold long to realize the quandary the Senior Planning Officer had found himself in. He would have been inclined in the first instance to turn down the request from Professor Agnew that Arnold be consulted by Alan Evesham. But that immediate reaction would have been tempered by a more considered reflection. There were other matters to take into account: the fact that Professor Agnew's brother was a councillor; the Professor's reputation and the consultancy work he undertook for the Morpeth Trust; and the public image of the Planning Department after the little-lamented departure of the previous Senior Planning Officer. So, the decision had been hedged. Arnold should be allowed a token activity-time off to meet Professor Evesham, but after that, work only in his own time, on whatever project Evesham was committed to. *And* try to bog Arnold down with work, so he would have neither opportunity nor inclination to spend much time digging away in the ruins of Northumberland's past.

'I thought you already had a pretty fair caseload,' George Sanders said. He was nicknamed 'Hollywood', but had no resemblance to the old actor whose name he bore. He was a balding individual of some thirty years of age, inclined towards gloom, and addicted to pinball machines which he attacked with ferocious concentration each evening in a local public house. He sat in his office now, scowling at the manila folder on the desk in front of him.

'I'd have said hefty, rather than fair,' Arnold suggested.

'Old Iron-Knickers trying to tie you down, I guess. He's come into this department like a breath of hydrogen sulphide.'

Arnold had no idea what hydrogen sulphide might be, but he could guess at the sentiment behind the remark. 'Is this the file on Kilgour Estates?'

'It is,' Sanders fingered the curling edge of the folder gloomily. 'Wouldn't have minded a few trips up into that area myself.'

'It'll require a visit?'

'More than that. A few, more's likely. You've got a purler here, Arnold, a real purler.'

'In what way?'

Sanders grimaced, displaying stained, tobacco-abused teeth. 'Like I said, I wouldn't have minded the trips out, but I was in no way keen to start. On the face of it, the application's more or less straightforward . . .'

'But . . . ?'

'There are problems.' Sanders sniffed noisily. 'To start with, there are several letters in the file — from people up there who aren't too happy with Patrick Yates.'

'Is he the applicant?'

'That's right. The owner of Kilgour Estates. Local magistrate, all that jazz, behaves like a country squire, you know what I mean. Hasn't gone down too well with some people . . . and with others, well they claim he's acted in a fashion you can argue is cavalier. I followed up one of the letter-writers . . .'

'Have you put a note on the file?'

Sanders wriggled dolefully. 'No, I didn't. The conversation became kind of . . . personal. I think, now you're taking the file, maybe you ought to see these people. There's certainly something weird about the whole thing.'

'Weird?'

'That's right. Maybe it's just me, but I get the impression that this guy Yates creates reactions in people that become a bit out of hand. I mean, from one source you hear he's got such a reputation for carnal pleasures that it won't be long before he needs to get fitted for plastic kneecaps; but someone else will tell you he's a raging queer.'

'And this is relevant to the planning application?' Arnold asked in wonderment.

'It is insofar as it tells you something about this character's personality and the effect he can have on people. The whole business is a can of worms and rather you than me.'

'What worms have you teased out so far?'

'A fat one. A lawsuit.'

'Oh dear.'

'Right.' Sanders clucked his tongue thoughtfully. 'One of the things exercising me was how I was to deal with a planning application from Yates when there was a lawsuit pending about his ownership of Kilgour Estates.'

'His ownership is in question?'

'He's got the deeds. But there's some guy who claims he's the rightful heir to Kilgour who's screaming about undue influence and wants the will that left Kilgour to Yates set aside.'

'How long has Yates held the property, then? Is this a recent development?'

Sanders grunted and pushed the file across the desk towards Arnold. 'He's been living on the property for about twenty years and has owned it — if that's the right word — for about three years. The claimant — he's called Bob Francis — also lives in the area now, but he emerged from the bush somewhere about eighteen months ago. A writer. Been out of touch, he says. Comes home to expectations and no realities. So he's trying the courts.'

Arnold picked up the file and weighed it thoughtfully in his left hand. 'How far has the lawsuit proceeded?'

'I think you're going to be lucky. My worries were to some extent unfounded. Chances are there'll be a decision within the next few weeks. This guy Francis, he had no money and it was going to be difficult to get legal aid. As far as I understand it, Francis would have had to take it to a judge in chambers who would pronounce on the likelihood of success. If the judge thought it was remote, Francis's case would have been thrown out. Poor Bob would then have had to slink back to his romantic hovel on the fell.'

'So what happened?'

'Ah, well, rather interesting. Suddenly poor Bob had money. Not quite certain where it came from. A mysterious benefactor. There's a village whisper that his wife is . . . shall we say . . . somewhat disenchanted and not willing to shell out any more of her own money to support his legal tantrums. But he's come up with the readies, even so, though exactly who the guardian angel might be . . . well, it's just rumour. Anyway, it all comes around to the fact that there *will* be a court hearing, full panoply of the law and all that jazz.'

Arnold frowned doubtfully. 'Do you think Francis has a case?'

'How the hell can *I* say?' Hollywood Sanders shook his head. 'I'm no lawyer. What I can say is I'm glad to get rid of the thing. Believe me, the whole business has something . . . *sniffy* about it, you know what I mean? So as far as I'm concerned, it's goodbye Charlie and good night.'

Which was little satisfaction to Arnold since he was left holding the file and the responsibilities that went with it.

3

It may well have been because of Sanders's concern about the 'sniffiness' of the Kilgour Estates business that Arnold seemed to find little time to start looking into the file. Sanders had injected a certain reluctance into Arnold as a result of his comments. Apart from that, however, while Arnold might normally have been tempted to take a quick look at the file over the first weekend — for he had rather too much on his desk for comfort at the moment — he also had Professor Evesham to think about. If he was to offer any serious assistance to the historian, it would be as well if he placed his knowledge of Ail the engineer on a sound footing.

Accordingly, Arnold visited the libraries in Durham and Newcastle Universities. He read all he could on the mediaeval masons and engineers. In Newcastle he managed to read — or at least, skim through — two of Evesham's own books on military history. At Durham he spent a few hours in the library at Castle Green and then afterwards mused on mediaeval building as he strolled alongside the river under the towering crag on which the university and castle stood.

It was buildings such as these that Ailnoth had built, in his peculiar pattern of endeavour: places of learning, locations for prayer, and symbols of strength, power and war.

But he had learned little new about Ailnoth: there was certainly no published link drawn between the engineer and the building supplier in the north of England.

He tried to get through his backlog of work in the early part of the following week. It was Thursday before he found time to pick up the Kilgour file. It was soon apparent that Sanders was right: there were several letters in the file that raised protestations which had little to do with the planning application itself. Rather, they were concerned with issues which Arnold regarded as peripheral. There were letters regarding the state of the tenant farms, and in particular there was one very abusive, occasionally obscene, and excessively bitter missive from a man called Enwright.

There was also one from the claimant to Kilgour Estates. The filed letter from Robert Francis was more moderate in tone. It was carefully typed and merely stated that, since he had an interest in the estate through the lawsuit against Patrick Yates, he contended no application for development at Kilgour should be contemplated by the planning authority. There was a long, rambling letter from someone called Winfield, detailing real or imagined grievances against the 'squire', but seemingly confusing the present owner Yates with the previous owner, Colonel Edridge. And there was the anonymous letter.

After Arnold read it he had doubts whether it should have been placed upon the file at all. It was scurrilous and in parts obscene. It was partly written, in a hand obviously disguised, and partly made up of printed words cut from magazines and newspapers. The accusations it contained ranged from underage defloration to bestiality. The writer clearly did not like Patrick Yates.

It was not clear whether the writer disapproved of the planning application.

There was a map attached to the filed application, Kilgour House lay north of Morpeth, in the Cheviots. It comprised some three and a half thousand acres. The sun was shining in Morpeth and Arnold decided it was time he went out to inspect the ground and discuss the application with Mr Yates, if that was possible.

The phone rang, unanswered. Arnold decided to drive out to Kilgour anyway, without an appointment fixed.

He left the car park at ten in the morning and took the A1 north, branching off after a few miles to plunge into the heart of the Northumbrian countryside. The route he took led him towards the towering mass of Cheviot, while to his right, as he crested rising foothills, he caught blue flashes of the seascape towards Bamburgh, distant pele towers crowning nearby crests, and a faint tang of salt in the wind from the coast.

For the next half-hour he drove through countryside familiar enough to him. There were the developed villages of thatched and stone-roofed cottages bordered by trim gardens hedged with box, still within commuting distance of Morpeth and Newcastle. Thereafter the hills loomed up ahead of him, the road twisted and turned back on itself and only when he breasted the next rise and saw the rich farmlands spread out along the lower slopes of Cheviot did the changes begin.

He had consulted the map and undertaken the detour from roads he knew well. The road dropped and a valley opened out ahead, dominated by a ridge outlined starkly against the backdrop of Northumberland hills crowned with fir and aspen and echoing to the cackling of black grouse. A stream ran through the valley, and the road followed its meandering; rich fields spread either side of the road for some two miles but then Arnold passed a dilapidated sign that seemed out of place. It bore the legend *ASH FARM*, but the chain supporting it was broken and it hung at an angle. The track diverting from the main road seemed overgrown and ill cared for. Half a mile further on he passed two cottages: trees grew against the base of the first and its crumbling walls seemed supported only by the strangling ivy that overran it.

The second cottage had been badly roofed with corrugated iron. Said iron was now rusted and flapping, while the cottage's wooden front door gaped on rusted hinges, with windows broken under the eaves above.

Arnold drove on, puzzled. The valley seemed prosperous enough, the land rich and capable of effective cultivation. He had caught a few glimpses of livestock, and there had been a tractor at work beyond the trees, yet as he drove further into the valley the signs of dilapidation and decay seemed to increase. He recalled the letter written by the man called Enwright: it had been abusive and Arnold had skimmed quickly through it for that reason. But the letter had been right about one thing: it had referred to the bad husbandry of the owner of Kilgour House, ascribing certain motivations to it, and while that was something Arnold could as yet have no views about, one thing was certainly clear: Enwright's remarks had some ring of truth. The tenant farms seemed rundown, decayed and abandoned.

It was an odd way for a prosperous estate with rich farming lands to be managed.

The village itself was tiny: a collection of ironstone cottages and a public house that looked large enough to serve the needs only of the village itself. There was an air of rural contentment about the place as it slumbered in the morning sunshine and the road that swung left, signposted *KILGOUR HOUSE*, was well metalled and the hedges were neatly shorn.

A half-mile on Arnold caught his first glimpse of the house itself. It lay at the foot of a steep bank crowned with larch and alder. The main building, built of warm brown and yellow sandstone, quarried in the West Midlands, testified to a Victorian builder who had wanted something different from the tough grits tones of the northern hills for his home. The main entrance was fronted with imposing steps and colonnades, a trifle flamboyant for Arnold's taste, but architecturally in keeping with the style and taste of the period in which it had been constructed. The west wing of Kilgour House was recessed, fronted by an ornamental garden which curved pleasingly towards an old carriage drive that must have been the main access point to the house a hundred years ago. At the end of the drive was an imposing set of wrought-iron gates, and beyond those the archway of Jacobean stables in a fine state of preservation.

The green lawns in front of the main house were bright and trim and the gardens were ablaze with colour. The stream cut through the trees on the right and fell into a natural basin fronting the house. A short distance away, overshadowed by an ancient oak whose mighty branches were supported by timber buttresses, there was an ornamental pool, half covered with lilies. The house was in no need of renovation: whatever decisions might have been taken with regard to the tenant farms further up the valley, they had had no application here. Kilgour House was in no need of repair: it had been well maintained, and sensitively repaired. Arnold's eye was keen but he could detect no unwise short cuts in the manner in which facings had been repaired, and no lack of vision in the way the entrance had been renovated.

Overall, Arnold approved.

He drove up to the house, swung towards the driveway and parked near the great oak in a spot he guessed would cause no obstruction. The sun was warm on his back as he walked up the steps to the main entrance, and on the grey slate roof of Kilgour House a blackbird sang a full-throated song.

The entrance was imposing, the bell a replica of an older Victorian iron version. The sound echoed inside and there was a short wait before the door was opened and a woman looked out.

She was in her mid-forties. Her hair was drawn back severely from her handsome features and lightly dusted with grey. Her eyes were of a startling blue, intense in colour and perception: the glance flicked over him and became dismissive. Arnold was not unused to making such early impressions. She stepped forward and the sunlight caught her skin: she was pale, as though she avoided the sun so that best advantage was gained of the blue tracery of veins under her skin. But such delicacy of impression was not echoed in her mouth: it held a marked determination, a conviction about what was right and wrong in her world. She was a handsome woman, and would have been a beautiful one but for the element of ruthlessness in her make-up which would always have deterred some men.

She frightened Arnold.

'Good morning,' he managed. 'My name's Landon. Is Mr Yates at home?'

'What is it you want with him?' The tone was cool, not impolite, but controlling events.

'I work for the planning authority. I thought it was time I came out to see him about his planning application and carry out a first inspection. I did phone in advance, but there was no answer.'

'No.' She considered Arnold, and the problem, her eyebrows drawing together delicately in a little frown of annoyance. She glanced around towards his car, and then nodded slowly, before stepping back into the hallway. 'You'd better come in.'

The hallway was magnificent. The oak panels were burnished gold; the echoing stone beneath their feet was polished, reflective of the high roof with its curved beams and the gallery that ran the length of one side of it. The woman was walking ahead of him, towards a room that would have once served as a morning room, Arnold guessed: he wondered what use this manor house would now have for such accommodation. The woman was wondering about other things: she paused in front of a full-length mirror against the morning-room entrance and inspected herself. Arnold gained the impression it was a calculated inspection that had little to do with female vanity: it was a checking that all was in order.

'Wait here,' she ordered, and entered the room after a light tap on the door. She closed the door behind her, leaving Arnold to contemplate the sun streaming in through the high latticed windows at the far end of the hall.

He walked towards the stairs. The timber was old and splendidly carved, curving up along the flight of stone steps to the first floor of the manor house. He guessed it predated the building of the house by perhaps a century: someone had cared for this house, enough to use the best materials, sensitively chosen. Now he thought about it, there had been a Newcastle builder called Connaught who had often undertaken commissions in the Northumbrian hinterland . . .

'Mr Landon.' Her voice was quiet, but positive. 'Mr Yates will see you.'

She stepped back into the room as Arnold approached hurriedly. She closed the door behind him and stood near it as Arnold advanced towards the man who had risen from the easy chair near the window where he had been taking advantage of the sunlight and the view over the hills.

'Mr Landon? I'm Patrick Yates.' He was extending his hand, his voice was courteous, but already Arnold was beginning to dislike him.

It was a condition in which he rarely found himself. Arnold was not given to making hasty judgements: long walks with his father in the northern hills, visiting ruined villages on the Yorkshire moors, being encouraged to look and touch, feel and think, had moulded his character in such a way that he tended to suspend judgements.

'Wait,' his father had suggested. 'Never jump to confusions.' The pun had been deliberate, and it was a precept that Arnold himself still held.

Yet there was something that he found immediately dislikeable in Patrick Yates.

In the fleeting moments of this meeting he tried swiftly to analyse what it might be. Yates was a stocky, well-built man with thinning hair and an elegantly tanned skin. His eyes were brown and gave the impression of warmth, though the warmth was somehow *skilled,* holding elements of professionalism that detracted from their apparent honesty. His heavy eyebrows were relaxed but his mouth was controlled: smiling now with an easy charm, but with a hint of doggedness at the corners that might mean Patrick Yates would brook no opposition to things he had decided on.

His handshake was firm, his manners practised, and though Arnold could not be certain what had caused his hackles to rise instinctively, he wondered whether it was because Yates's handsome features held something of the Dorian Gray about them. He was in his late fifties, Arnold guessed, yet there was something *younger* about him, an indefinable air that would make him attractive to young women and the despair of older ones who would wish for their own forgotten youth to return.

It might simply have been envy, but Arnold could not be sure.

'Pauline, is there any coffee available?' Yates asked.

The woman near the door nodded. There was a small table at her side. It supported a gleaming silver coffee-pot. She poured Arnold a black coffee at his request and brought it across to him, as Yates waved Arnold to the second easy chair near the window. He took it, and the coffee, vaguely aware that the cushion on the chair had been plumped up as though someone had recently been sitting there. Yates observed him coolly for a moment and then smiled. 'You won't really have been introduced to Pauline.'

'No.' Arnold struggled, wondering whether to rise.

'Pauline Callington. No, don't bother to get up, Mr Landon. She's my housekeeper.'

There was a tiny, bitten precision about the way he pronounced *housekeeper*. Inadvertently, Arnold looked up at the woman. She was staring at Patrick Yates. Her mouth was rigid and a muscle tensed briefly in her cheek before she brought it under control. There was a short silence as they looked at each other, Yates smiling softly, charmingly, the woman unmollified as the word hung in the air between them. The tension was palpable and Arnold could not guess at its cause. It was the man who held the whip hand, nevertheless. 'I don't think you need stay, Pauline. But thank you for the coffee.'

It was made to sound like an insult. She was unable to control the slow flush that stained her mouth and cheek. But there was iron in the woman. She inclined her head slightly, and without a word or a glance in Arnold's direction she turned and walked from the room. The door closed gently behind her.

Patrick Yates sighed. 'It's necessary, if one is to maintain relationships on an even keel, that certain things are made clear from time to time. Do you find that in your own circumstances, Mr Landon?'

Arnold sipped his black coffee. He was unwilling to be drawn, partly because he was not certain what the basic relationship between Yates and his housekeeper might be, and also because he was inclined to suggest there were ways of dealing with people other than insulting or humiliating them. But Yates's manners were not his business. Planning applications were. 'I've come to discuss your application, Mr Yates.'

'So I gathered. Do you see any problems?'

'In essence, no. Your proposals are to build an ornamental lake—'

'To replace that rather vulgar little pond in front of the house,' Yates said easily. 'It hardly sets off Kilgour, does it? Such a lovely house needs an appropriate setting.'

'Indeed. And the house *is* lovely.' If Yates thought so, he couldn't be all bad, Arnold thought. 'You also want to build a tennis court—'

'At the back of the house, that's right. It won't affect the outlook, or the external facade or the environs.'

'And certain improvements to the stables. The Jacobean stables—'

'Will be unaffected,' Yates interrupted, obviously slightly bored at the necessity to explain something that would have already appeared in the plans he had submitted. 'I want to undertake improvements in some new stable blocks and upgrade those I made available some five years ago.'

'They were cottages at the time.'

'That's right.'

'You obtained no planning permission.'

'I was not the owner, then.'

There was a curious, challenging inflection in Yates's last words, as though he was resisting an attack already repulsed once before. Arnold nodded. 'I don't wish to imply we'll be looking at that situation now. The fact is merely noted. I will need to look at the plans on the ground, however, and there are certain objections—'

'I'm aware of them. Under planning law, I don't see that you need to take any notice of them.'

'Aggrieved parties—'

'The Enwrights of this world don't classify as aggrieved parties,' Yates said sharply.

'There is also the matter of the lawsuit,' Arnold suggested quietly.

Yates's coffee cup clattered on the table as the man rose abruptly to stand in front of the window. He locked his hands behind his back and glared out across the lower meadow and the stream in front of the house to the rise of the hazy hills beyond.

'The lawsuit is rubbish. It doesn't stand a chance.'

'The lawyers—'

'Mr Landon, I was trained as a lawyer and I know what I'm talking about. The claim doesn't stand a cat in hell's chance!'

He brooded silently for a little while as Arnold sipped his coffee uneasily. 'You don't know much about this place, do you, Mr Landon?'

'No,' Arnold replied, subdued by the submerged ferocity in Yates's tone.

'It was built in the early years of the nineteenth century. The land was purchased by the Edridge family: industrialists from Staffordshire who sought the life of landed gentry for themselves and their sons up here in northern farming country.'

'There are worse places to live.'

Yates hardly seemed to hear him. 'They built the cottages to make the village about 1815, and they built this house. They cared for the place. They started a tradition, and their children followed that tradition. Life was placid, controlled, and good for more than a hundred years. But times change, Mr Landon, times change.'

'They do,' Arnold agreed unhappily and put down his empty cup.

'Colonel Edridge, as a young man, was keen to follow that tradition. He nurtured the idea and ideal of a continuous and protective ownership. I met him when he was about to retire from the Coldstream Guards. He wanted legal advice. We became friends. Eventually he asked me to become his estate manager. It was an attractive offer. I came twenty years ago. Kilgour House became my home.'

'It's a beautiful place.'

'Charles Edridge was an immensely sociable man who had a certain vision. He saw himself as part of a tradition in which a rural community of rural workers could flourish. His function was to form a link in a long chain. He'd hoped to found a dynasty, too. He married. A Swedish girl he'd met during the war. It didn't work. She was utterly incapable of providing him with the sort of love he needed, and they were divorced. Desertion.'

Arnold hardly cared to listen to the story: it was not relevant to his visit. But Yates was telling it as though there was some point he needed to make.

'The problem was,' Yates continued, 'if he could have no children of his own, how was he to deal with the estate?'

'Remarriage?'

'His experience with his wife had scarred him,' Yates said dismissively. 'But there was a first cousin, who had a son. They started a correspondence, and it seemed there was the chance that . . . You've got to understand, Landon, how a man like Charles could feel, if he was let down. There was a trust, you see. Certain financial problems arose in the late fifties. Charles borrowed against that trust. It was not, perhaps, wise. When I met Charles, I advised him on how to put it right. He had money available in the late sixties and it could be managed . . . but the cousin, he raised Cain. Caused problems. It cost Charles fifteen thousand pounds to settle, but worse than that, it embittered him against his own family. He wanted nothing more to do with them.'

'So the friendship with his cousin's son—'

'Ended,' Yates announced sharply. 'If Charles ever had seriously considered naming him as his heir, he certainly gave that up as an idea in the late 'sixties. They were not in touch. There was no correspondence. The man himself, once he grew up, made no attempt to get in touch.'

'We're talking of . . . Robert Francis,' Arnold suggested.

'The self-styled heir to Kilgour,' Yates sneered. 'He dropped out for years, a *writer* he called himself. He only crawled out of the woodwork again when he heard that the Colonel had died.'

'Leaving the estate to you?'

Yates turned his eyes in Arnold's direction. The glance was now cold. 'This has been my home for twenty years. I was Charles Edridge's closest friend. He had no other family. To whom else should he leave the estate? To a branch of the family that had let him down, abandoned him, *sued* him? I tell you, the man is a fortune-hunter, an impecunious rogue who wants to walk into a fortune he's never earned.'

'But which you have.' Arnold regretted the words as soon as he had spoken them, but Yates barely reacted. It was as though a personal, bitter anger was uncoiling inside him. Controlled normally, it was now moving like a slow deadly snake of hatred, taking over, directing the man's passions down a single, obsessive path that made him largely oblivious of his surroundings.

Arnold rose to his feet uncertainly. 'If we could have a word about the planning application—'

'I think maybe he's also behind the recent niggling about Ash Farm,' Yates interrupted, hardly seeming to have heard him. 'But when you get down to it, these people, they just don't know what farming is about, do they? Charles Edridge was not the greatest of farmers. When I came, the estate needed *managing*. And I turned it around. The basic problem was that the estate was too heavily tenanted. And the rents were uneconomic. So it makes sense — any sensible person would agree. What is necessary is to face reality, accept that a heavily tenanted estate is less productive than one where the owner takes the farms in hand. Do you know that in 1985 three-quarters of the let land put on the market in this country failed to find a buyer?'

'I wasn't—'

'Damn it all! It's far more profitable to allow a vacant tenanted farm to fall into ruin. What's the point of re-letting it and charging an uneconomic rent? Larger agricultural units are more cost-effective!'

And there was another reason which no doubt would have influenced the owner of Kilgour House — Edridge or Yates. If a tenancy was not re-let, once the tenants had gone the underlying value of the freehold property could rise at a considerable speed. The capacity of the owner to raise money on the vacant property would be greatly enhanced.

It was a policy that could help raise finance to build an ornamental lake and renovate old stables. But Arnold did not say so, for Patrick Yates was glaring at him and his mouth was set like a steel trap.

Arnold reminded himself he was at Kilgour to consider and investigate a planning application, not to take sides in an agricultural dispute.

Yates seemed disinclined to allow the conversation to end, however. 'I know what the story is, spread by people who are lazy, incompetent, and think the world at large owes them a living merely because they exist in it. I see enough of them when I'm sitting on the bench. When I was chosen as a magistrate some years ago I had views about life here in the country, and those views haven't changed. The North needs regeneration; the estates like Kilgour need hard work put into them. But it needs to be *unsentimental* work. On the bench I crack down hard on poaching: I know my views are unpopular — but I'm enforcing the law! Equally, if I'm to turn the estate around, make it the kind of place the Colonel always dreamed of, and bring it back to the prosperity it once enjoyed under the Edridge family, I have to make realistic decisions.'

Arnold cleared his throat, shuffled awkwardly on the spot. He didn't want to be on the receiving end of this harangue. He suspected that, while he might agree with the motives, he would not care for the consequential actions. 'The tenants—'

'A-hah! The tenants!' Yates's eyes gleamed angrily and his mouth was edged with a hard bitterness. 'I can guess what some of them will have been saying. They'll be pointing to the capital improvements that used to be made to their farms — and which have ceased during the last ten years or so. They'll be pointing to the three-year rent reviews I've instituted over that period, and they'll be saying that the rents have risen significantly each time. What *I* would say to you, Mr Landon, is: look at those rents. Compare them with the average nationally. And I challenge you to show me where Kilgour rents are above the national average. It's nothing more than the whining, bleating noises of a bunch of incompetents who have battened off this land for decades and are unwilling to face the harsh realities of the modern economy!'

The challenge was one Arnold was unwilling to accept. 'I'm sorry, Mr Yates, but all this is hardly my business. I'm here merely to carry out an inspection related to the planning application you've submitted.'

He had been unable to prevent the coolness entering his tone. Yates recognized it as a mark of disapproval, and his lip curled contemptuously. He was clearly beginning to regard Arnold as a member of the other camp. 'You'll have received letters, nevertheless, from the tenants. You'll need to give fair weight to my side of the story.'

'Letters have been received,' Arnold agreed cautiously, 'but as far as I can see they bear little relevance to the planning application and our powers in that respect. To that extent they will play no part in the decision — and it follows that our own discussion becomes . . . to that extent . . . tautological.'

Alarmed at his own boldness suddenly, Arnold ducked his head, mumbled that he needed now to carry out his inspection and requested Yates's permission to walk around the premises. Yates stared at him for several seconds, a frown marking his brow as he weighed up in his own mind the possible barriers that the planning officer from Morpeth might raise to his own view of the world. Then he nodded. 'Walk where you will. I'll say goodbye. There's no need for further conversation. If there's anything further you need to ask, it can be done by letter, I presume.'

Arnold was happy to escape the coldness of the room. The housekeeper, Pauline Callington, was standing in the hallway, fussing with a bowl of flowers. She didn't look the type to go in for extensive flower-arranging. Her eyes fixed on Arnold as he walked forward; they were hesitant, but calculating, and he thought she was going to let him walk past to the front doors without speaking, but at the last moment, she called his name.

'Mr Landon.'

'Mrs Callington?'

'I wouldn't want you to think . . .' She seemed flustered suddenly. It was as though she had something important to say to him but could not bring herself to say it. He waited. She shook her head, puzzled with herself. 'It's no matter . . .'

Arnold walked out into the warm sunshine. The blackbird had moved to a hedge of hawthorn but was still singing lustily. Behind the house a spreading chestnut was alive with creamy candles. The air was soft and warm, the hill was green and around Kilgour House there was an air of peace and quietude.

Arnold enjoyed his brief tour of the property. He looked at the Jacobean stables, inspected the ruined cottages that were to be converted, admired the sweep of the ornamental lake on the plans and checked where it would actually be built above the weedy, overgrown pond.

It was a beautiful location, here under the hill, with the fells rising green and brown and fading to a distant blue in the distance, and Kilgour House and its estates should have been a haven, a jewel in the northern farmlands.

The fact that it was edged with bitterness, plagued with quarrels and scarred with a long-standing dispute, based in ancient differences and conflicting viewpoints could not be ignored, however. Arnold sighed. It was a pity, a great pity.

But it was none of his business.

CHAPTER TWO

1

The arrangement Arnold had made with Alan Evesham to visit the village of Langton and its ruined castle had been somewhat indeterminate. On the Saturday morning, therefore, Arnold was surprised to receive a phone call from Evesham.

'What time will you pick me up?' Evesham asked abruptly.

'Pick you up?'

'To go to Langton. It won't take you far out of your way. I have a cottage in Ogle.'

Far out of my way, Arnold thought. Only about fifteen miles. 'I thought we'd be meeting at Langton itself,' he demurred.

'Can't. Dodgy motor. And old Agnew won't pick me up; says he's already up in the area overnight. Can give me a lift back, though, if *you* can manage to take me out with you.'

Reluctantly, feeling he had been cornered, Arnold agreed to pick up the Newcastle professor within the hour. He was not in the best of tempers when he drove away from his bungalow to make the cross-country run to Ogle. On the other hand, there was a certain curiosity stirring in him as he wondered what sort of cottage Evesham might have in Ogle.

It was a delightful surprise. At the end of the small village a narrow pack-horse bridge of some antiquity crossed the clear, stony stream and the track beyond, barely metalled, ran through hawthorn hedges to end in a small cluster of three cottages. All were old. One had certainly been originally constructed at the turn of the eighteenth century; in both of the others there were hints of earlier construction, and the timber braces in Evesham's cottage suggested to Arnold that it must have been the first cottage built in the tiny hamlet. He hadn't even been aware of the lane's existence at the end of Ogle village.

He told Evesham so.

The young professor seemed unimpressed. 'Swine of a place to live in. Have to have my own generator. No gas. Would never have lived here, but the place was left to me by a decrepit aunt, and it's cheap, commutable to Newcastle. When the bloody car's in shape. University dons are a depressed breed, Landon. Research cuts, salary cuts, don't know why we stick it.'

His general grumbling continued for several minutes while he sorted out various papers, including some old maps of the Langton area. He had expected Arnold to arrive within the hour, to keep their appointment with Professor Agnew at Langton, but he was not prepared to put himself out: he had waited until Arnold actually arrived before he stirred himself.

'Thought it was a good idea to invite Agnew to join us,' Evesham said. 'He's been moody about the research grant, and suggested involving you, so I thought I'd kill two birds. Get him to come along, see how important the research is, and show him I'm cooperating, dragging you in.'

Even if the dragging in was done reluctantly, Arnold thought. But the charmless Mr Evesham seemed unaware of any undertones of displeasure in Arnold's bearing. Perhaps he considered Arnold's feelings as beneath his notice, even if he had begged a lift from him in the car.

They left Ogle some fifteen minutes later than Arnold had intended, so he was forced to take the A1 north rather than use the narrower, more winding roads he would have preferred. Arnold disliked the A1. It was a good road and provided splendid views as it ran north, but even so, there were much more interesting highways crossing the hills and fells of Northumberland. They reached out into tiny, half-forgotten villages, the kind that clung to their past and hardly seemed to recognize the existence of the twentieth century — farming communities that still fed on their roots and heritage.

'I've done some more work on Ailnoth,' Evesham said, raising his voice against the noise of the engine. 'Got some more papers, copied from the Bodleian.'

Arnold swung in behind a trundling caravan to allow an urgent Jaguar to nose past him and accelerate away with a snarl. He checked his mirror carefully before pulling out to overtake the caravan himself. 'Did you discover anything new?'

'Very interesting,' Evesham bawled, his voice taking on a curiously high note. 'Seems he did some work at Winchester, on the King's Hall. Got a grant of timber for it. Six tree trunks — *festa* in the manuscript. It was by way of a payment for building the *verina,* the window frame of the hall.'

Arnold could not resist the comment. 'That might be a clerical mistake.'

'What?'

'*Verina* — window.'

'What the hell are you talking about?' Evesham asked irritably.

'I've come across a similar reading in an old manuscript — a building contract. The word was really *verna* — a windlass.'

'What the hell would he build a windlass in the Great Hall for?' Evesham demanded angrily.

But the seed had been sown. The don subsided unhappily, grumbling something under his breath, and leaving Arnold with the quiet, if childish, satisfaction of the thought that he had at least forced Evesham to reconsider his opinions and not regard them as sacrosanct.

At the first opportunity Arnold swung off the A1. He was heading along roads he had already travelled that week. Langton village lay only some five miles east of the Kilgour

Estates although the village did not fall as part of the land-holding of Patrick Yates. As they crossed the great ridge that ran up towards the Cheviots Arnold caught a glimpse of the head of the valley in which Kilgour House was situated, and almost as though Evesham read his thoughts, the Professor said, 'You ever come across that character Yates, of Kilgour?'

Surprised, Arnold nodded. 'I have, as a matter of fact. I was up there during the week, dealing with a planning matter.'

'Watch the bastard. He's poison. He's a magistrate, you know, but I'd like to see the swine hanged.'

'What dealings have *you* had with him?' Arnold asked.

'Bastard.' Evesham sniffed, and was silent for a while. 'I was involved about two years ago with some investigative work on Kilgour land. Wild scrub country really, no value to anyone, grazed by a few sheep and that was about it. I had material evidence from Northumberland records of the 1830s that there'd been a pele tower in the area — you know, one of those defensive towers put up to hold back the marauding Scots.'

'I know.'

'Could've been about 1228 . . .' Evesham muttered an obscenity. 'I took a dig out there. Alright, I didn't go through all the formalities like getting Yates's permission, but he turned up one morning and tried to bawl me out. In front of students. They were helping with the dig. I gave him as good as I got. Lost my temper. I admit to a short rein. He went white at some of the things I said to him. He was oafing on about trespass and me being no better than a poacher, so I told him a few home truths too. The girls in the party quite liked the womanizing bit.' Evesham chuckled unpleasantly. 'You pick up rumours in the common room. We've got a couple of senior profs who while their time away on the local bench. Yates, apparently, is an *active* bachelor — or used to be. I suggested those days were behind him. He changed from white to purple and then stomped off. You know what he did next?'

'What?'

'He blew the place up.'

Arnold swerved involuntarily. 'He *what?*'

'*He blew the bloody pele foundations to smithereens.*' Evesham's tone had changed: the malicious satisfaction was gone, to be replaced by a cold, edgy bitterness that Arnold found intimidating in its commitment. 'He could have just ordered us off, closed access to us. We'd have been annoyed about that . . . but that wouldn't have been enough for that vengeful bastard. At the weekend, when we were off site for the degree ceremonies at the university, he went up there, bulldozed down to the foundations, stuck a load of gelignite or some bloody stuff into the hole and carved a great gouge out of the hillside. It must have cost him a bit to do it, but it gave him great satisfaction. I stormed up there, to his bloody mansion, and bawled at him. He was cool as ice. Just told me it was his hill, he could do with it as he wanted, and now there was nothing there for me to dig for, there was no reason why I should trespass again.'

Arnold could feel the old anger rising again in Alan Evesham as wounds never scarred over bled again. 'I shouted at him,' Evesham continued, 'telling him he'd destroyed part of our heritage, but he didn't even laugh at me! It was just contempt . . . I almost went for him, but he had a bloody big mastiff at his side at the time.' Evesham fell silent for a while, but Arnold caught a tremble in the man's hands, clasped firmly on his knees. 'You saw in my study, that mediaeval pike?'

Arnold nodded. 'I did.'

'They used to use those pikes to stick heads on,' Evesham said coldly. 'As a warning, and as a punishment. That pike . . . it was just made for that bastard Yates's head. If I ever got the chance . . .'

Arnold was surprised at the over-reaction. He slowed as the car came over the hill and the lane narrowed. A farmer was ushering a small herd of cows across the roadway ahead of him, on their way to fresh pasture, so he stopped. Evesham was silent beside him, but there was a curious sound emerging from the man's throat. It was as though he were trying gently to clear his throat but the sound was a slow, continuous rumble, like a subdued growling. Arnold glanced at him. The man was oblivious: his eyes were on the cows ahead but Arnold was certain he did not see them. His eyes were fixed on a real past, now imagined; there might have been images of heads and pikes in that dream. Evesham's face had gained in colour, an unhealthy hue that matched the emotions he still clearly felt about the wanton destruction of a thirteenth-century pele tower.

Whatever had been said, and felt, and done in the brief relationship between Patrick Yates and Alan Evesham, it had left a suppurating sore on the Professor's emotions. 'We'll be at Langton soon,' Arnold offered.

The offer was rejected, and they drove the rest of the way in silence.

* * *

The village of Langton lay in a hollow. The cluster of cottages fronted a narrow village green bisected by a shallow stream in which five ducks paddled desultorily in the morning sunshine. At one edge of the village stood a converted farmhouse and barn, its modern reconstruction painfully insensitive to Arnold's eyes. On the rise beyond, a gravelled track led up to a yew hedge, past which could be seen the solid Norman tower of Langton church. As they drove down into the village Arnold's glance went to the crest of the hill: up there, behind the screening alder and birch, lay the remains of the controversial Langton Castle.

Parked outside the church were two cars, a dusty red Ford, and a battered old Buick that had seen long service abroad before it had ever been deposited in England. Arnold wondered at its history as he drove towards the church and parked his car beside the low grits tone wall.

Evesham got out of the car and without a word walked down the path towards the entrance to the church. Arnold stood for a moment, looking about him, smelling the wind from the distant sea, glancing towards the line of the fells and thinking about days long gone in the Yorkshire Dales of his youth. He turned and followed Evesham. The path was ill-tended, weeds growing in the interstices between the ancient stones, and the nettlewort and couch grass were rampant. He paused by a leaning headstone: wind and rain had eroded the words commemorating a death in 1880. It was not so long, Arnold thought, before oblivion.

Some attempt at repairs had been undertaken in the north-east corner of the churchyard. There was a certain raggedness about the effort that suggested untrained hands, and there was certainly a great deal to be done if the churchyard were to be properly tidied.

The interior of the church was cool and dim. It was a small church, a narrow strip of faded carpet gracing the entrance and leading towards a table on which were displayed a number of ineffectual appeal pamphlets. The pews were old, badly varnished in places and ill cared for. Arnold smoothed the old oak with his hand and grieved silently for it.

In the east wall were two stained-glass windows presented by long-gone families. At the transept, Arnold noted with a vague surprise, there was a stained-glass window depicting the martyrdom of St Stephen, presented by the Edridge family. He had not been aware that the Edridges of Kilgour would have seen Langton as their local church.

The two men standing near the font were now turning to acknowledge Alan Evesham. Arnold ambled down the church aisle in their direction. He recognized Professor Agnew, dark-suited as always, bald pate gleaming dully in the dim light, his great elephantine ears with their pendulous lobes drawing attention from his sharp little eyes and the prim mouth that hid an innate generosity of mind and spirit well known to Arnold and probably to Evesham too, in spite of the military historian's complaints about cuts in research grants of late.

'Mr Landon,' Agnew announced, stretching out a hand in welcome. 'I am appreciative that you could make it. I'm aware we're trespassing upon your valuable personal time. So pleased you are able to come along and offer us assistance.'

Alan Evesham glowered sullenly, annoyed that it was being suggested openly that he required assistance.

'May I present you to the vicar?' Agnew intoned. 'Mr Landon — Mr Barnack, vicar of Langton.'

Barnack was thin, thirtyish and thickening about the waist. He had a wispy moustache that he seemed to wish to hide for its ineffectuality, his left hand stroking it gingerly as though he wished it had never come. He was dressed in corduroy trousers and a turtle-necked sweater as though to emphasize that Saturdays were not part of his working week and he really was putting himself out for this meeting. Arnold guessed that whatever the state of the research grant fund, a generous contribution to Langton Church would be expected of, and given by, Professor Agnew.

He shook Barnack's hand: the grasp was limp, the skin damp. Barnack's eyes seemed oddly luminous in the dim light of the church, a deep-water creature unused to the sunlight on the hill. 'I'm pleased to meet you, Mr Landon,' he said unconvincingly .

Saturdays, Arnold thought, are Saturdays, after all.

'Mr Barnack hasn't been the incumbent here all that long,' Agnew said softly. 'We were discussing the state of the roof — his predecessor had made efforts, but not enough.' Decidedly, a generous contribution would be expected.

'I see some work has been done in the churchyard,' Arnold offered.

'Community Project,' Barnack explained. 'There was some money left over, apparently, and the county sent a supervisor and a few young unemployed people to start tidying up. I'm not certain it was an immense success, and when the money ran out . . .'

'It's a start, anyway,' Arnold suggested, after a short, heavy silence.

'Well,' Evesham said snappishly, 'We didn't come up here to waste time. Shall we go into the vestry?'

Professor Agnew glanced at Arnold. There was nothing in his expression that led Arnold to believe Agnew sympathized with him, but he suspected Agnew was grateful that Arnold was prepared to suffer Evesham's bad temper and worse manners at all. If not for too long.

Barnack led the way into the vestry. The room was narrow and cold. The old beech table was badly scarred at the edges; a thin cloth had been placed on its surface and a shaft of sunlight from the high window glanced down to illuminate the top volume of the three that had been placed on the cloth. There was a dark rich redness in the cover, deep under the encrusting dirt of age, and the faded leather at the corners had been badly worn, but the old records seemed to have been remarkably well preserved.

'They're not the original records, unfortunately,' the vicar was saying. 'These date from the sixteenth century. As far as I've been able to make out, there was a fire in the church about 1530. Records were damaged. An attempt was then made, over the following twenty years, to copy the fire-damaged material, but inevitably the work fell to several hands and the result is far from satisfactory.'

'That binding is older than 1530,' Arnold suggested.

'How do you know that?' Evesham asked sharply.

Arnold shrugged. 'I have a friend on the Quayside in Newcastle who is an antiquarian bookseller. He knows about such things. He's taught me a great deal. Those hinges—'

'Yes, yes, you're quite right,' Barnack said, glancing surreptitiously at his watch. 'It seems they did use older bindings, inserting new copies in with some original material. But that's as much as I know. Mr Evesham—'

'*Professor.*'

Barnack, slightly flustered by Evesham's correction, paused, glanced helplessly at Agnew for support, got none, and went on. 'Professor Evesham has already inspected these books with my permission. But I'm not sure what the purpose of this meeting this morning is. I'm here, I suppose, because two eminent gentlemen from the university have seen fit to visit the church here at Langton . . .' His voice died away, as his eyes sought out Arnold, concerned in some vague way that he might have upset his third visitor by not including him among the group of eminences, and perhaps worried he might have miscalculated by way of donation possibilities.

'Then let me explain,' Evesham butted in. 'I came here some months ago to follow up certain researches in military history at Langton Castle. I visited the church, checked the records, and found some interesting evidence that suggests a trace can be made upon the movements of a mediaeval mason and military engineer called Ailnoth. Even to the extent of perhaps showing that he was buried here in Langton Church.'

Barnack shuffled his feet uneasily. 'I'm not sure . . .'

'The relevant entries are here, Agnew,' Evesham interrupted. He moved to the second book in the pile, dragged it out and for the next two minutes scanned through the heavy, fragile pages with their faded brown stains, seeking for the entries he required. 'Here they are . . .'

Agnew pored over them briefly, sucking at his lips thoughtfully. At last he turned to Arnold. 'Perhaps you'd like to take a look, Mr Landon?'

Arnold peered at the book entries as Agnew stepped aside. He was vaguely aware of the hovering presence of Alan Evesham but ignored it as much as he could. In moments he was taken up by the beauty and age of the old pages, the stained materials, the crabbed, almost indecipherable scrawl of long-dead scribes who had laboriously copied the births and deaths and folk memories of men and women who were now dust.

'That's the specific one there,' Evesham said impatiently, stabbing with his finger at an entry in the left-hand column. The man was nervous: his finger left a small, sweaty stain on the manuscript.

'*Al . . . Iln* . . . it's difficult to make out,' Arnold said.

'I read it as *Alnith*,' Evesham said quickly. 'It's dog Latin, of course, and not too well scribed. But it reads *Alnith the controller*

— that's the meaning of *ordinantor,* just there — *Alnoth,* sorry *Alnith the controller interred September 5, 1187.*' Evesham's voice was shaky; his nervousness increasing. 'You see, Agnew, I think *Alnith the controller* was really Ailnoth the engineer.'

'The name's spelled differently,' Barnack interrupted.

Evesham glared at the vicar balefully. 'Read Shakespearean manuscripts. See how they didn't have common spellings even then, in the sixteenth century. Do you think they were particular in the twelfth?'

'But what's a controller?' Barnack responded. 'Is that the same as an engineer?'

Reluctance seeped into Evesham's tones. 'No. Not exactly, of course. But the thing is, Ailnoth the engineer was disgraced. My thesis is that he fell out of favour as an engineer and architect and was forced to another kind of business — a supplier of plaster, stone and tiles. He came north in that capacity. I think he combined his craft as a mason and engineer with that of a building contractor.'

'And controller?' Barnack insisted stubbornly.

'He would perhaps have been employing a number of men to do the building work.'

'It sounds . . . tenuous,' Professor Agnew suggested softly.

'No more tenuous than a number of theories constantly put forward in the physics and classical departments this term,' Evesham replied heatedly. 'I was amazed, for instance that you saw fit to offer 'support' to Armitage's project . . .'

Arnold's glance slipped away from the faded entry relating to Alnith the controller. He glanced along the lines above the entry and turned back a page. There was something wrong. He leaned forward, peering closely at the entries as Evesham committed himself to unwise criticism of Agnew's decisions on research grant placings in the university. In Arnold's experience you gained no credit for your own work by the criticism of others, but that was Evesham's problem, not his. He was becoming interested in the little puzzle that was unfolding in front of him: patiently, he worked back through the entries, turning the pages. At last he raised his head. 'Ah. I see now.'

The quiet satisfaction in his tone caused the heat to die between Evesham and Agnew. Professor Agnew turned his head. 'What do you see, Mr Landon?'

'The entries are out of sequence.'

There was a short silence. 'What does that mean?' Barnack asked.

'They're not consecutive. You said earlier that some of the records weren't originals — they were merely copies of older, fire-damaged sheets. Well, it seems to me that when the sixteenth-century scribe copied the entries and inserted the more recent sheets in among the old, before the volume was rebound in its old cover, he got some of the sheets mixed up.'

'Did you pick this up?' Agnew inquired of Evesham as he craned over Arnold's shoulder to take a look at the entries himself.

'I . . . I'm not sure . . . well, I read the entries, I don't think it really makes any difference about the order in which they appear,' Evesham replied lamely.

'You'll have been searching for specifics, of course,' Arnold suggested helpfully. 'I wasn't, of course. In such situations things tend to leap out at you more easily.'

'Not very careful research,' Agnew rumbled in a doubtful tone, 'if you don't even check upon entry sequence.'

'Time has been of the essence, you will recall,' Evesham replied, his voice rising in anger. 'I was being pressed . . . the research grant . . . and I don't see it makes much difference—'

'I'm not so sure about that,' Arnold said.

Evesham glared fiercely at him, furious at the interruption, and at what he suspected was to be further criticism of his research abilities and techniques. 'I'm not accustomed to having amateurs,' he sneered, *gifted* or not—'

'Why are you not so sure?' Agnew cut across him. 'What difference do you suggest it makes, Mr Landon?'

Arnold was silent for a little while, checking again the names, the dates of the entries, the difficult-to-decipher names and descriptions. 'Well, it's not for me to say, of course, for I have little experience in these matters. Even so, I find it interesting that so many people died within a few days of each other and were interred at this church.'

There was a short silence.

'I don't follow . . .' Evesham said, his anger dying, blanketed by his puzzlement. 'I didn't notice . . .'

'Because the entries were out of sequence, you didn't notice the sequence of interments. If you check, even quickly, as I did, you'll see that over perhaps a five-day period, according to the dates, there were something like eight interments. Rather a large number for a small parish like this one in the twelfth century.'

'A pestilence,' Barnack murmured. 'A famine . . . little children . . .'

'I don't think so. I can't read all the entries clearly, and I lack a classical education so I can't be sure of my translations. But I have picked up certain words in my own studies of the ancient building trades. Look, this entry . . . *Hugh,* buried on September 3, *Mapylton,* buried on the same day as the *Ilnith* entry, and *John Lobins,* interred on September 2. None of these were children.'

'Their ages are given?' Barnack asked.

Arnold shook his head. 'No. But that's probably because, as grown men, their ages were not known.'

'How do you know they were grown men?' Agnew asked, watching Arnold carefully.

'The dog Latin. I told you, I'm not skilled. But some words . . . this one here, a description of Mapylton, for instance. *Devysor.'*

'What's that mean?' Barnack asked.

Evesham cleared his throat. His tone was husky. 'It means a designer: a man who prepared the building designs from which masons carried out their work.'

'Master John Lobins, it seems,' Arnold added mildly, 'was the provider of *forme et molde.* I'm not clear what that means. But I do know what is meant by the term *dealbatores,* applied to *Hugh* and also to *Bennon,* interred the same day.'

'Let me see that,' Evesham said roughly and pushed his way past Agnew to pore over the book entries.

'I've had a classical education,' Professor Agnew said sombrely, 'but I've never come across the word *dealbator.*'

'There's little likelihood you would,' Arnold replied, 'other than by seeking out old building contracts. You see, when a building contract was drawn up, the masons responsible then had to draw together a working force. There were tilers and thatchers and carpenters — they were usually described as *helyers.* Then came the plumbers and glaziers, smiths and painters. Lower in the pecking order came the plasterers and pargetters. Perhaps lowest of all came those who supplied huts for the workmen who were building in stone and wood. The huts were made of wattle and daub. The men who built them tended also to be whitewashers. *Dealbatores.*'

'*Baldwin,*' Evesham gasped suddenly. '*Hottarius.*'

'A hodman,' Arnold said smugly. He was beginning to enjoy himself.

Alan Evesham moaned, a self-destructive, critical whine deep in his throat. 'Why didn't *I* see this?' he demanded. 'What the hell was I *thinking* of?'

There was a short silence, broken only by the harsh, frustrated rasping of Evesham's breath. Impervious to the presence of the others now, he feverishly scanned the pages of the records. Agnew watched him for several minutes, then turned gravely to Arnold. 'Do you think this is important?'

Arnold's eyes widened. He was no expert. He'd merely noticed something someone else had missed. 'Important . . . I'm not sure. Important to Professor Evesham? I suppose it . . . *could* be.'

Evesham's head half turned, reluctantly, away from the records. Arnold had an impression of one eye glinting hungrily in his direction. 'In what way,' Agnew continued, 'could this be important to Professor Evesham?'

Arnold considered the matter for a little while. 'I suppose . . . because he's trying to prove that Ailnoth the engineer is the *Alnith* here in the books at Langton. This could be helpful. The *Alnith* entry speaks only of the *ordinantor* or controller. But controller of what? The term was used of building works, certainly, but was it so used exclusively?'

'Go on.'

'Now the other entries are interesting because they speak of men who held particular jobs, descriptions certainly used in the building trade. This would serve to suggest that the ordinantor was one of the same group.'

Agnew frowned. 'The ice is thin—'

'But perhaps equally important is the fact of the dates of interment,' Arnold suggested.

'Why?'

'It suggests a local catastrophe.'

Evesham turned away from the records to stare at Arnold silently. Agnew glanced at him, permitted himself a wry smile, and looked back towards Arnold. 'It seems to me you already have the glimmerings of a theory.'

Arnold swallowed hard. He felt a quiver of excitement in his veins at the thought of the eminent Professor Agnew asking for instruction, and he was forced to admit the feeling of satisfaction that he now had Evesham's reluctant attention. The man was a boor; he needed taking down a peg or two. On the other hand, the ice was thin, As Agnew had already suggested . . .

'The Middle Ages was not the stay-at-home period that many people seem to think it was,' Arnold began. 'The fluidity of labour was really quite astonishing.'

'How do you mean?' Agnew asked, frowning.

'Stone buildings were rare. A small town would contain none but the church, or a nearby castle. The average town wouldn't provide sufficient employment for a considerable number of men in the building crafts: even modest building operations inevitably exhausted local supplies very quickly. That applied to skilled and unskilled labour. The result was considerable mobility of labour. For instance, a casual list of masons working in Windsor whose wages were in arrears in 1300 shows four each from London and Norfolk, and three from Lancashire, Shropshire and Hereford.'

'*Convocat latomos, architectos invitat*,' Evesham said hoarsely, '*cementarios et artis sculptoris . . .*'

'That, I believe,' Arnold said, 'was the Conqueror's command to build a great church for his abbey at Bury St Edmunds.'

Evesham's mouth snapped close like a steel trap.

'So workmen were drawn together for a building enterprise from some distances. It seems to me that the records we've been looking at suggest that some large building enterprise was certainly in train in this area in 1187. The people whose deaths are recorded here really tell us two things: first, that there was a group of people employed in the craft, working in the area at this time; second—'

'They could have been local,' Barnack objected.

'I doubt it, for reasons I've mentioned. Hodsmen, a designer, a whitewasher, a controller . . . no, the talent would simply not have been here in Northumberland.'

'You were about to state the second point,' Agnew said.

'Second, they all seem to have died in a common catastrophe.'

'A building accident?' Evesham asked surlily.

'Who can tell?' Arnold replied. 'But grown men, dying within days of each other, employed in the building trade . . . a fire, perhaps, people dying of their burns over the course of a few days — or a collapse of masonry, trapping the men, so that they were interred as they were found. And they would have been interred here at Langton wherever they came from for the simple reason that transport would not have been available to take them back to their home villages. Not in time, at least, before putrefaction set in.'

'I'm still not certain how this supports Professor Evesham's arguments about Ailnoth the engineer,' Agnew said slowly.

'Neither am I,' Arnold said. He shrugged cheerfully. 'But I must admit, that's not my problem. I'm only here to say what I see and what I know. There's one thing, though the records would seem to demonstrate that there was a man called Alnith — who might have been the Ailnoth Professor Evesham seeks — buried at Langton; that there was a building work of some consequence being carried on at Langton in 1187; and if only a link could be found between the Alnith and Ailnoth activities, the Professor has found the basis for his thesis.'

'What kind of link?' Agnew asked cautiously.

'That's not for me to say,' Arnold replied.

Mr Barnack, vicar of Langton Church cleared his throat, the possibility of a large donation looming ever closer. 'There is a local tradition, gentlemen. Perhaps I could remind you of it.' He gazed around at them benignly. 'It relates to the provenance of Langton Castle.'

2

The man who came walking up through the long grass of the hill meadow, skirting the copse to strike out along the path towards the castle ruins, was about fifty years of age. He was tall and lean, moving with an easy stride that suggested he was used to fell walking and would be fit for his age. He wore a tweed jacket, and his trousers were stuffed into heavy boots: as he came forward, he removed his battered hat to push back his thick grey hair before settling it back in place. His skin was weather-beaten, and as he came closer Arnold could see his eyes were brown, thoughtful, surrounded by the creasing caused by bright sunlight and searching fell winds.

At his heels moved a sheepdog, lean as its master, alert and careful.

'I thought I saw someone on the hill,' the man called out. 'Wondered what you might be up to.'

Mr Barnack made the introductions. 'Professor Agnew, Professor Evesham . . . ah . . . Mr . . . er . . . Landon . . . This is Tom Malling. Stalwart of the church fabric; owner of the farm on which Langton Castle now stands.'

'I'll agree to the latter,' Malling said, smiling. 'I'm not sure what you base the former description on, though.'

'Your recent donations have been most welcome, Mr Malling, even though you don't attend.'

The vicar clearly never lost sight of his objectives.

'So what brings you gentlemen up to Langton?' Malling asked.

The vicar had already explained down below in the coolness of the church. There had been some dispute about the date when Langton Castle was first built; the dispute had dragged on for years. Waters had been considerably muddied during the 1830s when some enthusiastic amateurs had started a dig on the site. They had destroyed more evidence than they found, to support the thesis that the castle had been constructed as late as 1330. The learned articles they had then written had later been reproduced in part in the County History series: *that* accolade had given half-baked theories a certain credence, and it had proved remarkably difficult to unseat the argument, even though it was clear that while there certainly had been a castle built there in 1450, much of the 'original' work had in fact been constructed in 1720 by an enthusiastic Lady Glynne-Stuyvesant whose passion had been the creation of romantic ruins a little before the practice became really fashionable. She had the money to do it: she built them, knocked them down until they resembled ancient ruins, and then had her portrait painted against the gloomy, lowering backgrounds they presented.

Lady Glynne-Stuyvesant was not beloved by historians, although there was no doubt she had considerably aroused lay interest in ancient castles and even older abbeys.

'Ah,' Tom Malling said quietly. 'Lady Glynne-Stuyvesant. Yes, she certainly did confuse things. Even so, I think there's still some evidence that there was *something* here in the fourteenth century.'

'You're interested in old buildings?' Arnold asked.

The brown eyes dwelled on him for a few moments, summing him up. Malling smiled. 'Not really. I like looking into some matters of antiquity, but really, it's just because Langton Castle lies upon my land. I come up here sometimes in the evening. It's a lonely place, and quiet, and you can let your mind range. The past comes back to you then. It even achieves a sort of reality for now, if you know what I mean.'

Arnold did. He understood Tom Malling perfectly. From where they stood now they had an unbroken view across the hills of Northumberland, the fold of the land below them allowing them to see for thirty miles or more. Today, with the sunshine, there was a certain haziness, particularly out towards the coast, and the scudding clouds, white and grey against the sharp blue of the sky, seemed to accentuate the distance and open up the horizon.

But with a mackerel evening sky, and the soft warmth of an evening in high summer in Northumberland, Arnold knew the atmosphere up here would be quite different. The ruins of the castle would play their part of course, as romantic ruins had always played their part for Lady Glynne-Stuyvesant. But the backdrop of the hills would change — they would shade darkly against the evening sky lending an air of mystery. The cry of a wandering barn owl would add to the solitude, where the lights of the village below would be hidden by the slope, and under the deep dark summer blue of the northern night sky, memories would take over. The ancient knowledge of the hill would stir, uncurling slowly under the stars, until anyone sitting up here would feel only the stilled hush of the meadow, hear only the soft whisper of lives long ended, and recognize again the importance to the present of what had occurred in the past.

Tom Malling was staring at him.

The man seemed shaken, disturbed at something he had seen in Arnold's face. It was as though Arnold's thoughts had been communicated to him to strike some responsive feelings deep inside Malling's own head. The confusion in the farmer's eyes was caused by the shock of recognition and by an unwillingness to accept how close another human being could be to him, responding to his thoughts, feeling as he felt. Arnold himself was vaguely disturbed: he and this stranger were brothers under the skin, it seemed, and it was not a feeling he could accept entirely. Both men hardened a resistance that was reluctant, but real. Both felt a vulnerability they resented.

'Well,' Professor Agnew was saying, 'there's little enough to go on here at the castle itself.'

The west wall was still standing to a height of some fifteen feet, the stones pitted and scarred by time. The east side had been clumsily rebuilt — possibly by the indefatigable Lady Glynne-Stuyvesant, Arnold guessed, but the remainder of the castle had been levelled over the centuries. The keep was a grassy mound — attempts at excavation had clearly been made in the past but abandoned. It would probably have been a wooden structure anyway, Arnold guessed, inside the safety of the stone walls. Elsewhere, the perimeter wall was visible only as footings, some of which had been excavated, the rest appearing merely as craggy stones peeping through the rough, sheep-cropped turf.

'A romantic ruin,' Mr Barnack said cheerfully. 'But who knows what secrets it might reveal?'

Surprisingly, Professor Agnew, to Evesham's clearly expressed disgust, turned to Arnold. 'What do *you* feel about it?'

Taken aback, Arnold shook his head. 'I'm not sure. I mean, I'm not clear what I'm supposed to be looking for. The castle, well, it's been messed about with so much it seems to me a major dig would be required before you could ascertain with any degree of certainty whether it had really been erected in the time of Ailnoth. And even then, that doesn't prove that Ailnoth was involved.'

'But if we could prove that building works *were* being carried on,' Alan Evesham interrupted, 'we could argue the case for funding to carry out the dig. And it needn't be as expensive as all that: I'm sure we could pinpoint the *likely* position of the ancient works—'

'Expensive, extensive, that's all very well,' Agnew said, scratching his elephantine left ear, 'but you know the state of the budget.' Arnold thought he detected the beginning of impatience in Professor Agnew's tones. 'The faculty budget is limited. Government cuts . . .'

Arnold stepped away. This was nothing to do with him. He had the suspicion that, although Agnew had his problems with his budgets, he had also had problems in the past with Professor Evesham, and was not averse to getting his own back by withholding funds at this juncture. Although, Arnold concluded, there was a certain justification: the evidence for Ailnoth's presence in Northumberland was pretty slim, and he couldn't see that it was particularly important anyway.

Aware that Barnack was engaging Malling in earnest consultation, no doubt attempting to increase his benefactor's bounty, Arnold walked away along the crest of the hill. Malling's dog watched him for a moment, then, after a brief hesitation, took a parallel course, watching Arnold as he would an errant sheep, ensuring it made no break from the flock. Amused, Arnold extended his hand welcomingly: the dog's ears flattened against its head and its belly dropped closer to the ground. It watched him, and he walked on, and it came closer.

The western wall of the castle had commanded a view in the old days that would have extended across to the Cumbrian fells. The ruins of Hadrian's Wall would have been a source for quarried material, no doubt. Below the west wall was a steep drop, although Arnold guessed from the line of the land that in earlier days the castle might have embraced the ridge some three hundred feet below. The shepherd's wall might well have an earlier history, for the ridge itself had a man-made look about it.

Something touched Arnold's leg. The sheepdog had decided he was trustworthy. Arnold sat down on a craggy rock and scratched the dog behind its ear. Below him a jay fluttered in the trees, scolding something in the scrubby undergrowth.

For a while he contemplated the horizon of the hills, allowing his mind to drift, to contemplate the past and recall the days when his father had shown him the countryside in the Yorkshire Dales and explained to him the heritage that had been left to them, stone and wood and tree. But gradually something else began to intrude. Arnold had always admitted to curiosity, and it was now aroused, almost subconsciously, for although he was not concentrating, something was intruding, an annoyance, an excrescence upon his unconscious mind.

Something was out of place.

As soon as he became aware of the feeling he looked about him. Within a matter of seconds he knew what it was. His mind and eye had become attuned to nature — man-made structures intruded. And within the copse of trees below him there was certainly evidence of old activity.

He rose, the dog starting up swiftly beside him. Arnold descended the crag; the path was narrow but short, and he was quickly in the alder and young birch. The dog snuffled behind him as he pushed his way through the trees until he reached the mound, and the broken walls.

They were old, and they had served over the years as material for the walls on the slopes below. There was little to be seen as Arnold moved slowly around the ancient structure. In no place was it more than three feet high, and most of it had vanished altogether. Below the inner perimeter of the castle defences, it could well have suffered from siege.

'*Landon!*'

It was Alan Evesham. Arnold raised his hand in response. 'What are you doing down there?' Evesham shouted. 'There's nothing of any interest there!'

Not to you, perhaps, Arnold thought. 'I'm just poking around,' he satisfied himself by saying.

'Professor Agnew has to get back. He's offered me a lift. He suggests we meet again in the week, to discuss possibilities. I'll give you a ring, to let you know when.'

If I can make it, Arnold thought sourly. He turned away, just as the lean figure of Tom Malling appeared on the skyline.

He wandered around the perimeter of the building, struggling through the trees at some points. He grew confused, not certain whether he had lost the line of the foundations and he stopped, puzzled. The dog whimpered and he looked back: Tom Malling was descending the crag. The dog's body quivered, the tail swinging rhythmically. Tom Malling pushed his way through the trees to join Arnold.

'You seem to have made a friend of Sally.'

'She's friendly enough.'

'Not to all strangers. You seem to have . . . made an impact.'

Malling was frowning slightly, as though he was still affected by the moments up above on the hill. He glanced around him. 'You've found the chapel, then.'

'Chapel?'

'That's right. When Langton Castle was restored by Lady Glynne-Stuyvesant they came across the outer perimeter of the castle. Much of it destroyed, of course. Farmers like me.'

'The needs of the land.'

'I suppose so. Anyway, the existence of the chapel here would suggest the castle was bigger than the good lady had at first realized. I think it took some of the wind out of her financial sails, too. Or so it's suggested in the County History.'

'Not the most impeccable source of accurate information.'

'Is that so?'

'I'm afraid it is. Enthusiastic Victorian historians had a tendency to indulge their imaginations and make situations fit their theories. To suggest this was a chapel, for instance . . .'

'You don't think it was?'

'Would you build your chapel outside the walls?' Arnold asked.

'Inside the *outer* walls,' Malling replied.

Arnold looked above them to the crag and shook his head doubtfully. 'I'm not so sure. Why build an outer wall down here? Professor Evesham might be able to tell us, since he's a military historian, but I would have thought that this area here would be fairly vulnerable to attack. It would have been well served for water — the spring over there which will have carved out that gully — and the area is levelled as though there have been gardens here . . . Yes, it may have been part of the outer grounds of the castle with the defensive inner wall surrounding the keep, but a chapel?'

'Maybe a chapel for the peasants out here, with another for the gentry inside?' Malling suggested.

Arnold smiled. 'It's possible. But, if this was a chapel for the poor, it was rather large, wasn't it?'

Malling looked around him and nodded. 'I suppose so. I hadn't thought about it, really. Can't say I'm exactly into old buildings — though the farm itself is pretty old.' He stopped suddenly and looked carefully at Arnold. 'From what they were saying up above you seem to know a lot about the way people used to build in the old days.'

'I'm interested.'

'And a lot about the way they lived?'

'I have certain limitations in that respect,' Arnold said vaguely, his attention beginning to wander from what Malling was saying to something he had seen in the walls to his left, shadowed by the trees. 'I suppose I know a fair bit about the building industry over the years, working as they did in wood at first, then stone . . . Excuse me . . .'

He edged away from the farmer and approached the ruined stone at the edge of the copse. He crouched down, staring closely at the stone, and he shook his head.

'What's the matter?' Malling asked, coming up close behind him.

'I'm not sure,' Arnold said hesitantly. 'It's just . . . odd, I suppose.'

'In what way?'

'Look at this here. It's brick.'

'*Brick?*' Malling leaned forward, inspected the thin piece of walling. 'Brick in a building this old?'

Arnold smiled. 'It was the Romans who introduced brick into England. They were more like tiles than modern bricks, of course, but their thinness enabled them to be very

66

well burned. That's the principal reason for their remarkable durability.'

'Are you saying that . . . brick there, it's Roman?'

Arnold straightened, frowning. 'I think so. But there's something odd about its colour, here. I can't just think . . .'

'But the Romans surely wouldn't have built a chapel here.'

'I'm not suggesting that. Remember, just as shepherds raided the wall for material for their pens, so it would be quite possible that others could have raided Chesters for instance, to take brick to incorporate into their own later buildings. It was quite common, you see, for masons in Roman times and later, to use bricks for bonding courses. They inserted them at intervals into flint or stone rubble masonry.' He shook his head. 'But that doesn't entirely explain . . . I'm not sure.'

'So you know a lot about the masons of older times then Mr Landon . . . What are you doing about lunch?'

3

Arnold followed Malling's directions: the farm lay a half-mile across the fields but some three miles by the detour of the road which Arnold had to take by car. They parted on the hill. Some fifteen minutes later Arnold drove along the winding lane that opened out into the track that dropped alarmingly down to the brook, the tiny bridge, and then the gateway to the farm.

The farmhouse itself nestled under the hill, protected by a bank of birch and horse chestnut, and the farmlands seemed well cared for and relatively prosperous, if somewhat given over, for EEC subsidy purposes, to the growing of rape. The farmhouse was typical of the area, bearing signs of an eighteenth-century structure built upon something rather older. As he grew nearer to the house he could in fact make out a brick-patterned sign that announced the building of the house in 1692.

Malling was waiting at the gate.

The garden through which Arnold passed was small and dilapidated. It seemed it had been laid out years ago, probably with flowerbeds, but they had deteriorated and were overgrown and weed-infested. Malling caught Arnold's glance. 'I have a woman comes in three times a week. She doesn't turn a hand to gardening.'

He led the way down the stone-flagged passageway into the kitchen. Clearly, Tom Malling lived a bachelor existence. There were few signs of a woman's hand. The curtains were feminine enough, but faded, and there was a general air of untidiness about the place which suggested to Arnold that the three-times-a-week hired help didn't turn a hand to clearing away, either.

Bread, cheese, an apple and a can of lager were offered and gratefully accepted. 'I hope you didn't expect a three-course meal,' Malling said.

'This *is* three courses.'

'There's more lager.'

'I wouldn't mind a can,' Arnold said. 'But I also wouldn't mind paying a call first.'

'Top of the stairs.'

Arnold walked back down the passageway to the stairs and made his way up over the worn stair-carpet. On the landing he paused, irresolutely, faced by two doors. He tried the first one and realized he had made a mistake. It was a bedroom. He paused, about to close the door, and then was struck by the fustiness of its atmosphere.

It was dimly lit, the curtains still drawn and it had a dusty stillness about it that suggested it had not been used for a long time. The bed was made up but, in marked contrast to the kitchen, everything was neatly placed. It was an unlived-in room, he felt, and something prickled at the back of his neck. There were three photographs on the chest of drawers that faced him. They were of the same woman, but he could make them out only dimly.

Softly he closed the door and tried the door next to it. This time he was right: it was the bathroom.

Tom Malling was standing by the kitchen window when he returned, a can of lager in his hand. He turned as Arnold entered. 'I got another drink for you from the fridge.'

'Thank you.' Arnold sat down.

Malling watched him for a moment. 'This thing about the bricks up at Langton Castle. You know a lot about such things?'

Arnold had the feeling the man really wanted to talk about something else, but was seeking a roundabout, less threatening approach. Though what the threat might be, Arnold had no idea.

'I know there are many misconceptions about bricks and their use.'

'This house, for instance,' Malling said, waving his hand. 'Can you tell me anything about it from the bricks used?'

Arnold nodded. 'I could. I have to admit, I'd be cheating if I didn't tell you I'd already seen the date of the house — 1692. But even if I hadn't I could have told you its date, roughly. It's an example of one of the later trodden bricks. They stopped using them at the turn of the century — few examples after 1710.'

'Trodden bricks?'

'A primitive method of manufacture. They dug out suitable earth. Trod it out on a piece of hard ground laid with straw. The treading of the clay was done in bare feet: they had to do it that way to make sure they got out all the pebbles, otherwise the clay would split or crack in the firing. They chopped up the clay in convenient sizes, laid them out to dry, prayed there'd be no rain and then they burned the bricks.'

'I see.'

'Sizes of bricks weren't regulated until 1571 with the moulds they developed. These are certainly standard sizes.'

'Not like the ones up at Langton.'

The conversation was moving, but slowly, a stately galleon manoeuvring through difficult, unknown waters. It wasn't Langton Castle Malling wanted to talk about.

'No, not like the ones at Langton. They are . . . well, a bit of a puzzle. You see, when the Romans left, brickmaking, died, in effect, in England. The tiles and bricks could still be cannibalized, of course, and that's maybe where the brick at Langton came from. But I can't be sure. There's something about it . . . I'll have to read some books again. There are plenty of examples of hard Roman brick being re-used, not least for the angles in church towers . . .' Arnold fell silent for a few moments, struck by an elusive thought. It was gone before he could hold on to it. 'Anyway, although there was plenty of great brick building in Italy, France and Germany in the twelfth century, like St Sernin at Toulouse, we've got very little in England. We built mainly in flint . . .'

'Hmmm.' Malling sipped at his lager. 'From what I gathered in the conversation at the castle, however, it's military history they're really on about.'

'Something like that.'

'So why are you brought in?'

Arnold hesitated, for some inexplicable reason unwilling to explain himself. 'I'm not sure, really.'

'I gathered it's because of your knowledge of the ancient building craft.'

'That's part of it.'

'So you know all about the masons, then, do you?'

'I'm not sure—'

'Professor Evesham, when he was arguing with Professor Agnew, he said something about the drawing together of the building crafts into Langton, and that you supported the argument — or had even advanced it.' Malling took another sip of lager, but it was almost as though he was calming himself, suppressing further some subdued excitement. 'So what was that all about?'

Arnold shrugged. 'Nothing very significant, really. Fairly common knowledge. A shortage of skilled and unskilled labour in mediaeval times meant they had to bring together, from quite a wide area, the skilled people they needed to undertake a building programme of any size. In stone, anyway.'

'And that's what happened at Langton?'

'Of that, I'm not sure,' Arnold replied cautiously. 'It's a possibility. The deaths in the area, the interments, they suggest—'

'If they *did* all come here to work on the castle — and that now seems something Professor Evesham will be clinging to, do you think they will have formed a secret society? A gild?'

Malling's eyes seemed to glitter feverishly suddenly. Arnold was held by the ferocity of the glance: it seemed *important* to Tom Malling that the fact should be determined.

Arnold shook his head. 'I doubt it.'

'Why?'

'As far as I'm aware, it was really from the beginning or the thirteenth century that industry was organized in a system of craft gilds. It's true such gilds were strictly local — the fact that a man was a member of a craft fraternity in one town gave him no right to practise the craft in another.'

'But building workers . . . the *masons* . . . they were different.'

'Not so,' Arnold disputed. 'I admit that local gilds would be unsuitable for masons because they were on the move so much, from one part of England to another. That led to the formation of permanent gilds for some trades, but temporary associations—'

'The *lodges*,' Malling interrupted, almost sneering.

'That's right, associations centring upon the lodges or workshops where they were employed. But that wouldn't have happened here. We're talking of a gap of maybe a hundred years or more. But why are you interested?'

The banked-down fires in Malling's eyes died slowly. He look a long, careful sip at his can of lager. 'I'm not, really. I suppose I was just taken aback at the possibility that a craft gild of masons might have actually been established on my property.'

'It didn't happen.' Arnold hesitated. 'But what if it had I mean, what difference does it make?'

'None, I suppose.' Malling managed a tight little smile. 'It's just that . . . well, I dislike masons—'

'You mean freemasonry.'

'Yes. When I look around me . . . there are evenings when I go up to the castle and just sit, staring out over the hills in the darkness. I think you know what I mean . . . feel what I've felt . . . This has been a great country but it has been brought to its knees by something rotten at its core. In my view that rotten thing is freemasonry. It claims to have Christian links but is anathema to the Christian Church; it claims to exist for good but is afraid to show its face in the light of day, clinging to secret practices; it argues that it is based upon ethical moral codes that have been developed over the centuries, but it is in reality a web of corruption and secret dealing, where every brother seeks to make the best advantage for himself and his colleagues in the society. Freemasonry is corruption, Mr Landon.'

Arnold frowned, staring at the can of lager in front of him. He was unwilling to be drawn into this discussion, although he had the vague suspicion that this was why he had been invited to lunch with Malling. The man surprised him: the balanced, open-air farmer he had met on the hill had taken on a brooding vehemence accentuated by the unbalanced view he seemed to take of life and society, and the controlled ferocity with which he had spoken suggested banked fires of resentment inside him ready to rage uncontrollably at the slightest opportunity.

Arnold was also aware of a twinge of resentment: at Langton Castle both he and Malling had felt they had something in common. He now believed it had been a mistake. He had little in common with Malling, other than the realization of the depth and wealth of their heritage, summed up on a summer evening on the hill.

Defensively, Arnold said, 'I think that's somewhat exaggerating things. You may well be right, to some degree. I have no real opinion or feeling about the matter. But you shouldn't confuse the mason's gilds with freemasonry.'

'I remember reading, Mr Landon, that no less an authority than Wycliffe once condemned the gilds.'

Arnold nodded. 'I can quote you. He denounced the new Kilds, the *men of sutel craft*, because they conspired together so that no man of the craft should work for less than any other.'

'A trade union which became corrupted by power developed in secret.'

'I think you've still not understood the crucial break in the link between mediaeval gilds and modern freemasonry. The travelling masons went to the lodges in the fifteenth century and made themselves known to the master in charge by a particular form of salutation.'

'A special handgrip.'

Arnold nodded. 'The secret handgrip is the only thing one can describe as a solid foundation for the erection of the vague and fantastic temple which later writers built to enshrine the mysteries of an occult freemasonry. Believe me, Mr Malling, as far as the available evidence goes, there is simply nothing to show that modern philosophical freemasonry has its roots in the mediaeval craft masonry. The first hint of "freemasonry" appears in a fifteenth-century rhymed treatise, but it contains no mystical peculiarities. Freemasonry is in fact an independent seventeenth-century growth. The mystical ritual wasn't really adopted until as late as 1773. The truth is, the whole thing was grafted on to the craft. It used its technical terms in a symbolic fashion. Nothing more.'

'But the gilds *were* secret. They were not to reveal what was done in the lodge,' Malling insisted.

'There was no doubt an *element* of secrecy about the craft,' Arnold admitted, 'and there is a superficial similarity also in the fact that skilled men possessed a knowledge of geometry at a time when all science, however elementary, savoured of magic. It's easy to understand how the gilds became surrounded by an air of mystery. But there is no real connection: the later body merely took over the words and symbols. There it ends.'

Tom Malling nodded, somewhat abstractedly. The glitter in his eyes had died, and he seemed calmer, almost relieved in some peculiar way by what Arnold had said. 'You may well be right. Freemasonry is evil . . . but the ancient craft gilds, from my understanding, had certain good things about them. The sworn masons, for instance . . .'

'You know about sworn masons?' Arnold asked in surprise.

Malling stared at him vaguely. 'I once read about Richard atte Chirche. It was in an old book, in the reference library . . .'

'The *Liber Albus*, perhaps.'

'It's possible.' Malling stared at his empty can of lager and nodded. 'Yes, they were responsible people. It's good to know that the connection between the crafts and the freemasons is tenuous, or even fraudulent . . .' He paused. 'It's a matter of little importance, I suppose, but I just had the feeling it would be ironic, feeling the way I do about the corrupt influences of the freemasons, that on my land there should have grown a gild to which freemasonry owed its origins.'

Arnold frowned. He watched Tom Malling warily. The comment suggested to him that the obsessions he had already detected in the farmer ran deeper than he had realized. Malling was a man given to over-reaction. The external person seemed controlled, balanced, equable in nature and friendly in temperament. But he was scarred inside by obsessive influences. Arnold remembered the bedroom upstairs, the fustiness of a room not used in years, the photographs of the woman in the dimness. And then there was his first impression of the house, with its old, untended garden, a flower garden of the kind a woman might have built and a man allowed to decay . . .

Impulsively he blurted out, 'You have a woman who comes in to clean, Mr Malling, but have you never married?'

There was a short silence. Malling continued to stare at the empty lager can. Then, silently, he rose and moved towards the door. Arnold rose also, feeling the blood drain from his cheeks, aware he had been guilty of a blatant and unwarranted intrusion into someone else's personal life. Malling led the way down the short passageway to the front door. He opened it and stepped out into the sunshine. He raised his head, looked at the sky, sniffed at the wind. 'It'll be a fine afternoon.'

'Yes,' Arnold agreed, subdued. 'Thanks for the lunch. I'd better be making my way back to the office now.'

There was a short silence. Somewhere up on the hill where Langton Castle stood, rooks cawed raucously, disturbed by something or someone. Malling turned to look vaguely at Arnold, and something painful moved deep in his eyes, a long slow crawl of an unforgotten agony. 'I did marry,' he said.

Arnold made no reply, not knowing what to say, unhappy now that he'd even been so crass as to raise the subject.

'We lived in Cambridgeshire then,' Malling went on. 'Came north to this farm after we married. Isabel loved this land and so did I. We were happy. I thought that . . .' He grimaced suddenly, and his lips twisted as though there was a bitter taste on his tongue. 'She died . . .' He pondered the words, frowning, then shook his head, as though he rejected them as inaccurate. Arnold gained the impression that Malling was struggling within himself, forcing himself to accept a recollected reality rather than a myth. 'No . . . she committed suicide. It would be four years ago, now . . .'

Silence fell around them. The rooks were quiet, and the hills seemed to brood above the farmhouse, dwelling on the words Malling had uttered. Arnold began to understand. There were unspoken things between them, but he was now aware of what the empty bedroom with its old photographs might mean. The obsession with things of little importance to this farm, even though they might have wider social consequences, was an escape, a route Tom Malling took to avoid the painful personal things that affected him. To concentrate his venom and bitterness upon freemasonry meant that he could avoid turning inward to gnaw over the things that really hurt him, the loss of his wife, words that might have been said and perhaps never were, the sad detritus of regret that lay whispering like dried leaves in every man's mind when he contemplated the past and what the future might have held, had things turned out differently. Arnold thought of the vigils at Langton Castle.

'I'm sorry,' he said awkwardly. 'Life must be . . . lonely.'

Malling blinked. 'I manage,' he said crisply.

'I'm sorry, I didn't mean to imply . . .' Miserably, embarrassed, Arnold made things worse. 'It's just that I know neighbours can be no substitute for—'

'Neighbours!' Tom Malling almost spat out the word. 'Don't talk to me about neighbours! Or the Church. Mealy-mouthed words from the pulpit, explanations about holy ground being unsullied by suicides, sly sniggers in the village. Hypocrisy and guilt, Mr Landon, these are the things which make up a village community. There is much evil in this world, and it needs extirpation. The ancient gilds had it right, perhaps.'

Arnold frowned. 'I don't follow—'

'The word neighbour,' Malling interrupted fiercely, changing tack, 'should mean friend, but when I look about me, in the village, and in the hills . . .' Malling half turned, looked out across the fells. Arnold stared with him, not certain what the farmer was looking at.

'Neighbours . . . There's at least one needs hanging,' Malling said in a soft, almost gentle tone, somehow the more chilling for its restraint. 'And one I'd quite cheerfully hang.'

But it was not until he was driving away from Langton village that Arnold realized Tom Malling, when he spoke, had stared towards the head of the valley in which Kilgour House was situated.

CHAPTER THREE

1

The Senior Planning Officer swivelled in his chair so that only his profile was presented to Arnold.

He was a large man, comfortably built, with a paunch that suggested it was pleasure rather than necessity that dictated his eating habits. This was in marked contrast to his predecessor, whose digestion was under permanent attack from his wife's cooking.

The new man was, like Arnold, a bachelor, however, and clearly in control of his gastronomic juices. He was rather less in control of his personality, which seemed to slip in and out of gear like a manic cuckoo clock. It was a matter for puzzled discussion in the office as to how he had managed to get this job — his interview must have taken place on a day when his star was in the ascendant. It was not that the office doubted his paper qualifications, or his experience for that matter: it was merely that he seemed to have been promoted beyond his capabilities in that, however good a planning officer he might have been, he seemed incapable of dealing with people.

Constitutionally incapable, Arnold considered. The man simply found himself uncomfortable when dealing with members of the human race. The profile was an example of the problem. It was not that the Senior Planning Officer had a Barrymore complex because someone had once told him he had a perfectly handsome, classical profile, it was merely that this way he did not need to meet Arnold's glance. The more serious symptom was that it was impossible to see him without an appointment, and when an appointment was made he was almost always out, called away on urgent business.

Communication was by memoranda: terse, grudging, and precise.

Consequently, it was with a feeling of surprise that Arnold found himself summoned to the Presence. As the Senior Planning Officer stared nervously out of the window, Arnold looked about him noting the changes that had taken place in the room since its last occupancy. It was lighter, fresh wallpaper had been added of a kind unusual in the Morpeth offices, there were two framed Degas prints and a rather ineffectual watercolour of a Devon tor arranged on the wall behind the desk, and the curtains on the window were pastel shades with pretty flowers. And now that he had time to note more closely the Senior Planning Officer's appearance, Arnold became aware of the elegant grey suit and immaculate white shirt and blue tie, the carefully shaved nape of the neck, and the precise parting in the smooth greying hair. The Senior Planning Officer was a careful, fastidious man. Arnold wondered how he would manage when trouble came.

It would seem the Senior Planning Officer considered trouble had already come.

'Mr Landon,' he intoned in a modulated voice that had been developed against a shaving mirror, Arnold guessed, to check upon its weight, balance and moisture content. 'I've called you to my office to discuss a serious matter.'

Arnold believed it. So did the rest of the planning office. The silence grew. Arnold was unwilling to break it. At last the Senior Planning Officer sighed and raised his profile a trifle. 'It's this Kilgour thing,' he said distastefully. 'There's been another letter.'

He gestured vaguely towards his desk. He showed an inch of cuff, precisely. Fascinated, Arnold was forced to drag his glance away towards the letter on the desk. 'Sir?'

'It's from that man Francis,' the Senior Planning Officer offered. 'He's threatening legal action against the department. Can he really do that, Mr Landon?'

'I'm not sure, sir. I mean, it's something that could better be answered by the Department of Administration.'

'This is a *planning* matter, Landon,' the Senior Planning Officer insisted sharply. 'There's no need to drag in the Administration people with their legal language. We must show we are capable of maintaining our own house in apple-pie order: no need to go running every time a problem arises. We must deal with it ourselves!'

What he really meant was Arnold must deal with it, of course. Arnold sighed. 'Of course. I merely meant, if it was a legal matter, it should be dealt—'

'This man is suing the owner of Kilgour House. That much is clear. But now he's saying that we should not treat the application from Mr Yates, or deal with it in any way, until the hearing of the lawsuit is completed. That could take months, Landon, years even. We all know,' he added gloomily, 'how dilatory lawyers can be. It's how they make their money.'

'I don't know how far the lawsuit has proceeded.'

'Then you need to find out, Landon, you need to find out,' the Senior Planning Officer said snappishly, clearly giving the impression he considered himself surrounded by an idiot clan. 'You're assigned to this application from Kilgour House and we certainly can't have the Francis fellow hauling the department into the courts. So forestall him, man. Find out what can be done.'

'I'm not sure how I can do that, sir.'

The Senior Planning Officer was faced with the same conundrum. He placed the tips of his elegant fingers together and a small wrinkle appeared at the side of his mouth as he began to whistle, gently and nervously. This interview had already gone on too long to suit his nervous disposition:

soon, he would begin to sweat. 'Well . . .' he murmured desperately, 'do what you can, man, do what you can. Go see this fellow. *Persuade* him.'

'Persuade him to do what, sir?'

The chair tilted irritably. 'Would you leave me now, Landon? I have another appointment.'

As he left the room Arnold noted that the appointments diary on the Senior Planning Officer's desk had a virgin, unsullied appearance. Nevertheless, Arnold had his instructions. He was to do what he could. He was to persuade the litigious Mr Francis.

'Persuade him to do what?' Hollywood Sanders sympathized. 'Pull back from his bloody action against Yates? No chance. He's virulent. Apart from that, it's none of our business, is it? Yates has put in a planning application. He's being sued by Francis. What's that got to do with us?'

'I suppose we could argue we have a *locus standi*,' Arnold suggested miserably. 'Right to appear in court as an interested party.'

'Try that on,' Sanders warned, 'and you'll have the Administration Department wallahs down on you like a ton of bricks. They got the lawyers; they like to do the court work.'

'But the Senior Planning Officer doesn't want them involved. It's a matter of departmental pride.'

'Bloody baronies, that's what we all work in. No one pulls together: each department jealously watching the others, buzzards over a piece of raw horsemeat.'

'It's an unusual way of looking at the public interest,' Arnold suggested.

Hollywood Sanders sniffed. 'Maybe so. But don't cross our Chief Buzzard for the sake of keeping your nose clean with Chief Buzzard Administration. Really want my advice, Arnold?'

'Please.'

'There's a new guy just joined us. Thorley. Green and fresh as a spring meadow. Hand the file to him.'

'The Senior Planning Officer—'

'Will never know. Until it's too late. And do you think he'd have the guts to bawl you out?'

Arnold was forced to admit he was tempted, but he shook his head. It would not be fair on young Thorley. 'I'll have to deal with it myself.'

'You're a nice guy, Arnold. *Stupid*, but nice.' Hollywood Sanders shook his head. 'You won't go far. But then, which of us will? Planning, like life, is a dangerous business — and one that none of us ever survives. Now isn't that a philosophical thought, Arnold?'

It was, but it didn't help Arnold to a solution.

* * *

The threatening letter from Mr Francis lay on his desk for several days. It was terse and to the point.

Dear Sir,

You will be aware that an action is pending between the writer and Mr Patrick Yates concerning the disputed ownership of the Kilgour Estates.

Should action be taken on the planning application submitted by the said Mr Yates, your department will be joined as a party to the action, and you will be held responsible for any works undertaken on the property to the detriment of the writer.

Yours faithfully,
R Francis

Arnold was not sure whether Francis had taken legal advice before writing the letter. It smacked of bluff, and a certain misunderstanding of the legalities involved. As far as the planning department was concerned, Patrick Yates was the duly registered owner of the estates and that was that, lawsuit or no lawsuit. On the other hand, the letter constituted notice, of a sort. Perhaps the best way out of the situation, Arnold concluded, was to do precisely what the Senior Planning Officer had suggested. *Persuade* Mr Francis. To what course of action? That was another matter. Nevertheless, Arnold clung to the word *persuade* like a terrified parachutist. It might bring him safely to earth.

A visit to see, and talk to, the letter-writer was clearly necessary.

For the third time in two weeks Arnold took the road north from Morpeth towards Kilgour, Langton, and the sweeping rise of the Cheviot foothills.

The address on the letter had demanded a check on the map, and a chat with one of the older members of the planning department who knew the area well. Armed with detailed instructions Arnold set out from the office and looked for the coppiced hill above Langton that he had been warned about.

The sky was a shifting pattern of scudding clouds and the hills were clearly edged, the hint of rain in the air magnifying them slightly. The road was quiet and Arnold drove at a steady pace. When the coppice loomed up ahead he slowed, waiting for the turn-off: it was as well he had closely heeded the directions, otherwise he would have missed the narrow road that ran through the arched, deserted railway tunnel and branched left along the old track towards the cottage that lay half a mile on.

It was set under the overgrown hill that had once been a railway embankment. The cottage itself had started life as a tiny railway booking office: part of it had been demolished but the cottage itself had been renovated to some extent, though never finished. The roof was good, and the sitting room and bedroom above seemed in sound order but the sagging stone to the right of the doorway in which the woman stood suggested that major structural repairs were required if the cottage was to remain habitable.

The woman was dressed to go out. She wore a light, belted raincoat. She was perhaps in her early forties, fair-haired, and her features were of a faded prettiness that had become marred by dissatisfaction. There was a petulance about her mouth that suggested to Arnold that she felt herself ill-used by the world, and the manner in which she used the cigarette in her left hand made him consider that anger and resentment would be one of the principal emotions that moved her.

As he stopped the car near the cottage she came forward.

She was frowning, staring at him as though he did not measure up to her expectations, whatever they might have been.

'I was expecting a removals van,' she asserted with the belligerence of disappointment.

There seemed little Arnold could answer to the comment so he got out of the car awkwardly and said, 'This is Station Cottage?'

Her glance was sharp; it flicked over him like a paring knife, removed a slice for dissection and then discarded it. 'You didn't see a van on your way up here?'

'I'm sorry, I didn't.' Arnold hesitated. 'I'm actually looking for Mr Francis.'

It registered. The sharpness in her eyes was blunted for a moment, and then she looked at him again, warily. 'What do you want with him?'

'Is he here?'

'I'm Mrs Francis.'

They stood staring at each other as though preparing for conflict. Arnold could not understand the edge of tension that had already built up between them: she seemed resentful, and yet curious. He was unwilling to give her any information he didn't need to, but could not explain the feeling. It was as though he suspected she might use information as a sword, a method of attack.

'My name's Landon. I'm a planning officer at Morpeth.' She was unimpressed. Her eyes said so.

'Your husband wrote to us,' Arnold tried again. 'I thought I'd better talk to him about it.'

'I wouldn't know what he'd write to you about,' she said, almost indifferently.

'It's about the lawsuit he has pending against Mr Patrick Yates.'

'*Christ!*' she said, and half turned away, thrusting the cigarette to her lips and drawing at it angrily.

'I take it he's not in at the moment,' Arnold suggested.

'Not at the moment, and not recently,' Mrs Francis said viciously. She stared at the cigarette for a moment, then dropped it, ground it out with her heel. Arnold was left with the impression she wished it was her husband's face. 'And I know sod all about what he's been writing you about. Not about that, and not about anything. Fact is, Mr Landon, I've had enough. The bastard walked out yesterday and it's taken him long enough to make a decision. I should have walked out on him years ago and would have done if I'd had any sense. But I really thought when we came here things would change, that maybe we could get it together again, you know what I mean? Build our relationship, at the same time as we built this place together. *Build*! God, look at this place! I put my money into it, you know, and now the bastard's walked out! You sure you didn't see that bloody van?'

Arnold shook his head, embarrassed. 'I'm sorry, no, Er . . . the letter we had . . . it used Station Cottage as the address, Will Mr Francis be returning here?'

'When I'm gone?' She gave a harsh, barking sound that bore little resemblance to a laugh. 'Not bloody likely, it was my money, and that penniless bastard is getting nothing out of it. He's walked out and that's it. I'm closing down, moving out, and this goes on the market straight away. And he won't get his grubby fingers on a penny of it. So there's no chance he'll be getting back in here.'

The words she used about her husband bore little reflection of the image Arnold had of him at a distance. He had thought of him as the potential heir to a large estate, and this had clearly coloured his judgement. Unless that of Mrs Francis was completely soured. Perhaps something of his thoughts found echoes in her mind for she sneered suddenly, shaking her head. 'Planning officer, hey? He's been writing to you. And it's about that business over the lawsuit. Yes, you already said that, didn't you?' Her mouth was bitter, wry with the taste of resentment. 'That lawsuit, it's pie in the sky. Nephew of old Edridge he might have been, but he never cared a fig for the old man, any more than he cared for me. He married me because I could give him security and he only tried to crawl back into Edridge's favour when he found that it would cost him if he didn't. He doesn't stand a cat in hell's chance in that lawsuit and I hope he gets ripped to pieces by those shyster lawyers they employ in the courts. I want him to get shown up for the seedy bastard he really is.' She glared at him, thrusting her dislike of her husband into an overall hatred of all things male. 'I don't think I can help you, Mr Landon.'

'Thank you, Mrs Francis. I don't think you can. Unless you know where your husband can be contacted.'

'In hell, eventually. Until then, I couldn't care less.'

Arnold nodded and got back into his car. He reversed across the narrow lane with difficulty and manoeuvred the car to return the way he had come. Mrs Francis watched sourly from the doorway of Station Cottage. As he slipped into first gear to drive away she called out to him, 'And if you see that bloody removals van, stir the lazy bastard to get up here!'

Arnold wondered what she had been like when the missing Mr Francis had first married her.

As he drove down the old railway track he considered it was likely he had had a wasted journey. He checked his watch. By the time he drove back to Morpeth the office would be closed. He had no idea where Francis had gone to, of course, but village life being what it was, it was quite possible that information would be available if he asked in the right area. He drove towards Langton village. Barnack might be new, but vicars were usually recipients of information — and gossip.

The road looped over the hill past the coppice, and within a mile or so he was back on the main road that ran into Langton. Behind him was the valley where Kilgour lay. It made Arnold think again of Tom Malling and something crossed his mind briefly, a comment Malling had made. There was something Arnold had found interesting, something he had meant to dwell on, perhaps look into further. The thought danced elusively away — something that was happening to him more and more these days, he thought gloomily. Advancing age; the approach of senility.

There was something going on at Langton village.

The ruins of Langton Castle crowned the hill, and the church nestled below, above the cluster of cottages and the pub and the small village shops. To the left of the village was an open meadow, and on it several marquees had been erected. Several trestle tables were placed to the right of the marquees and most of the population of the village seemed to be scattered around the area. Arnold caught the flash of sunlight on metal as the clouds above parted briefly and sunshine flooded the village. Then the road dropped, he lost sight of the meadow and he turned past the village shops to climb up towards the church.

The vicarage was a dour, uncompromising building with blackened stone and two blind windows on the north side, one with a head of cusped ogee form. Arnold observed it as he waited for an answer to the doorbell. When the door opened it was Mr Barnack himself who stood there.

'Ah Mr Barnack . . . I wonder whether you can help me.'

'Of course, Mr Landon. That's what I'm on earth for.' Barnack said blandly. He brushed some crumbs from his dingy-coloured sweater as he spoke and the slight bulge in his cheek suggested to Arnold the vicar was halfway through a late lunch.

'I've just been up to Station Cottage to look for Mr Francis.'

'Oh yes.'

'He wasn't there.'

'Ah.'

'His wife told me he'd . . . left home. She didn't say why but I got the impression that the . . . er . . . domestic strife was of some long standing.'

'And you thought that perhaps information regarding this unhappy state of affairs might have reached my ears?'

'Something like that. I just wondered . . . would you know where I might locate Mr Francis?'

Barnack assumed an owlish look. Perhaps he thought it made him look wise. In fact, he merely appeared bemused by the sunlight. Heavily, he said, 'One does hear various pieces of information about local people, of course, but gossip . . .

'I just want to know where he's moved to, so I can make contact. The fact is, he wrote to us, and the address given was Station Cottage, but—'

Barnack nodded sagely, accustomed to the vagaries and wanderings of his flock. 'He was not there. Yes well as I say, it is hardly my function to dispense gossip in the village. Equally, it is my function to render assistance where I am able. So, if I can satisfy one situation without offending the other I am happy to do so.'

Arnold waited.

'Of course,' Barnack continued smugly, 'while I am not really prepared to hazard a guess where Mr Francis might now be . . . ah . . . *living,* Since I have no confirmation of the *fact,* I am certainly in a position to suggest to you where he *might* be this afternoon.'

Arnold sighed. 'And where might that be?'

'With the toxophilites,' Barnack intoned, making the group sound like a remote Christian sect.

'Archery?'

'The village is holding its fete this afternoon. An occasion for celebration which I always feel holds something vaguely pagan — in its roots, you know? However, all are gathered at Long Meadow this afternoon. You must have seen them as you entered the village. I suggest you go there, Mr Landon. It's more than possible Mr Francis will be present.'

'He's interested in archery?'

'Somewhere there,' Barnack said with a self-satisfied grin, 'I seem to detect a *non-sequitur.*' With every sign of enjoyment and anticipation he began to close the door. 'Let me simply add that he has friends who are interested and as for Mr Francis . . . he does have a certain *macho* image to uphold . . .'

* * *

Whatever the incumbent of Langton Church might feel about village fetes and their possibly pagan origins — though Arnold suspected that Langton fete owed its conception to the 1930s rather than the 1300s — the villagers themselves seemed determined to enjoy the occasion. The entrance to Long Meadow was festooned with fluttering flags of all colours. A ruddy-faced farmer's daughter stood by a deal table at the entrance to the field collecting entrance money, and in the far end beyond the marquees a whistling and booming and cranking rattle pronounced the existence of a steam engine with its gathering of enthusiasts.

On the trestle tables that he had noticed there were scattered various field events, ranging from Find the Lady to jumble sales. A local schoolmaster sat in some rudimentary stocks for his pupils to send usually ill-directed tomatoes and wet sponges at him, and in one of the marquees a noisy game of bingo was inevitably under way.

The largest of the marquees was being used as a refreshment tent and several matrons stood at its entrance, sipping tea from paper cups. Children whooped around and, from the loudspeakers slung among the bunting, a recent pop song blared out, disregarded by all and sundry.

The archery enthusiasts were tucked away between the first and second marquees, with a demonstration area facing away from the main part of the fete, down towards the brook at the far end of Long Meadow. There were several barrels of beer nearby, and a dozen men partaking of refreshment. Arnold wondered about that, in view of the array of weapons present.

He was surprised by the weapons, as he drew near. He had perhaps expected to see the kinds of bows and arrows that were used in films and television plays and from time to time in shop window displays. But as he looked around he realized this was a much more serious business than he had imagined. The weapons here on display were of a varied kind. There were some recognizable items that seemed to have been modelled on the old clothyards that were familiar to him from ancient manuscripts. On the other hand, there were modern varieties that owed more to science and technology than anything else. One glittering monster was being used for demonstration purposes. Arnold stood and watched for a few minutes as the muscular young man with the dark, curly hair and narrow lips flexed his muscles and brought the silently whirring aluminium cams at the bow tips into action. He was stocky but well-built. His short-sleeved shirt clung tightly to his powerful upper body and arms, and he clearly took pride in his gear and the bow he used. The leather guard on his arm, protecting the forearm against bowstring burns, was supple and gleaming, his green and brown camouflaged kit looked clean and new, and everything about him seemed to demonstrate sharpness and commitment.

Arnold didn't like his mouth: the sharpness and commitment were there too, and as he sent the broadhead arrow towards the target Arnold felt the man would have preferred a live target.

'About £350,' a woman's voice stated just behind him.

Arnold turned.

She was perhaps thirty years old, her dark hair cut short, her skin tanned by wind and sun, her clear eyes the palest blue imaginable. She was of medium height and slimly built, but the slimness was muscular, her hips and thighs powerful and strong, her breasts firm. She too wore a leather guard on her arm, and she carried a modern bow, although it was clearly not as expensive as the one wielded by the curly-haired man.

'Who is he?' Arnold asked.

'Nick Enwright,' she replied, hardly glancing at Arnold. 'Bit of a nutcase, really. I mean, £350! Mine cost me a hundred quid and it's good enough — and I'm committed. But Nick behaves as though he's in the bloody jungle. It's like he believes anything that moves is fair game and so he's got to have a machine that'll knock over whatever comes within range. He doesn't seem to realize we don't get too many elk, whitetail or mule deer around here. What he'd really like is black bear. But in Northumberland? And you don't see too many shark off the Farne Islands — and seals don't move fast enough to make fair game.'

'He actually goes hunting?'

The woman looked at him quickly, as though she felt she had been talking out of turn, exposing thoughts that should have remained unspoken. She looked Arnold over, perhaps aware of him for the first time. She showed in her glance that she thought him unworthy of anxiety and she smiled vaguely. 'Who knows? Better ask the magistrates.'

She moved away and Arnold watched her go. An attractive walk, an attractive body. Her features were a little hard, perhaps, and maybe she was putting too much effort into her athletic image, but he guessed she would be a determined, positive woman with a mind of her own.

Even if there was a hint of envy in her words and the way she looked at the man called Enwright.

Arnold moved on. Ranged along one of the trestle tables was a selection of magazines and books, competing with the table next to it which carried second-hand gear for the enthusiastic toxophilite. Arnold briefly scanned the cult magazines stuffed with information, advertisements for bows and arrows, leather guards, information about equipment and technical articles about drawstring weights and pulling power, cable guards, calibrations and stabilizers. When he saw articles about blood trails and multi-blade broad heads he gave up and moved on, to look at ex-Vietnam Camo jackets and bottles of doe-in-rut urine, 'guaranteed to lure bucks within shooting distance'.

'The lunatic fringe, Landon. It isn't what archery is all about.'

Arnold recognized the sharp tone before he turned. He was surprised momentarily, but then his surprise quickly evaporated. A meeting of this kind was not entirely illogical for a man with a passion for military history and an interest in mediaeval weapons.

'Professor Evesham. Good afternoon.'

Alan Evesham was dressed in a light jacket and oatmeal coloured trousers. He was certainly not prepared to undertake any shooting but the evil-looking crossbow he carried in his arms was probably not intended for actual use, but rather as part of a display.

'I've got a stack of stuff in the car,' Evesham confirmed. 'There's a mediaeval section in the display in the marquee. Some interesting stuff there. I've got a few items which will surprise them.'

'You're not an archer, though?'

Evesham hesitated. 'I've done some shooting. I've even used this one a few times. And I am a member of the club, though I don't go in for some of the nonsenses of the real enthusiasts. Still, hardly imagined *you* were interested. Hidden depths, Landon.'

'I'm afraid I've misled you. I've no interest in archery.'

The veneer of vague cordiality that had overlain Evesham's manner slid away, its sheen rapidly disappearing at the Professor's realization that Arnold was here by chance. 'I see. Just been poking around at the castle: hey? Have you got anything new to help? I saw you wandering off around the chapel, but I can't imagine you'll find anything significant there.'

'I'm not sure you're correct in calling it a chapel. Surely, as a military historian, you'd assume the building lay in an indefensible position?'

'Outside the inner wall?' Evesham shrugged. 'Not unusual. Of course . . .' His voice died away as he pondered on the matter. Irritation took over. Arnold guessed it was occasioned by the thought that once again an amateur was trying to tell an expert what he should have known in the first place. 'Don't see what importance it can be anyway,'

Evesham argued. 'The thing is, a building which post-dates the period we're interested in can hardly be expected to reveal much in our search for Ailnoth.'

'There are Roman tiles in that structure.'

Evesham stared at him belligerently. 'So?'

'I . . . I'm not sure. But the matter needs investigating.'

'And that's what you've been up there for today? Waste of time.'

'Actually, I haven't been up to the castle at all today.'

'But you said—'

'No, Professor Evesham,' Arnold interrupted quietly, 'you said. I've been looking for someone. I was told by Mr Barnack that he might possibly be here.'

'At the demonstration?' Evesham glowered about him. 'Most of the damned village is here, that's for sure. Who you looking for?'

'A Mr Francis, from Station Cottage.'

'Don't know him,' Evesham announced and walked brusquely away.

Irritated by Evesham's rudeness, Arnold strolled around the perimeter of the display. It was quite possible Francis was here, but there was no way Arnold would be able to discover him in this throng. Nor indeed did he feel he really wanted to be bothered any longer. He found the atmosphere in the Long Meadow vaguely disturbing. It was supposed to be a demonstration of toxophily, of weapons old and new. The object was to recruit to the club, clearly, and contests had been arranged for people at various stages in skills development, including a small school for children. But there were vague, almost indefinable overtones which Arnold found distasteful. The young man with the curly hair and the muscles was still flexing his powerful bow in front of an admiring audience, and at a small group to his left a tall man with a grey-flecked, neatly-trimmed beard was holding forth to a small audience about a safari he had undertaken in Kenya.

'The fact is, even the Wata, the legendary elephant hunters of the south, have to use deadly toxins. They can draw bows a white man couldn't even bend but arrow power alone is not enough to stop dangerous game. On my second safari I brought down a buffalo. I also got two antelope and a couple of guinea fowl. Of course, when I took the guinea fowl I abandoned the hollow tubes of light alloy: for that prey it's enough to use wooden arrows without sharp pointed tips. I mean, the impact of the arrow itself is enough to pierce small game . . .'

Bombast, Arnold thought, and strolled on.

He was not enjoying the afternoon. He really had better things to do than stand around listening to people who were not clear whether they were Crécy-orientated or Sherwood-Green-fixated, artists or killers. Nor did he care generally for fetes as a whole. Clusters of people noisily determined to enjoy themselves, tended to make him shrink away. The hills were clean and the air clear and he could have been walking above Rothbury Crags and seeing the hovering falcon rather than wasting his time here in Long Meadow, among the cacophony he disliked.

'I'm surprised to see *you* here, Mr Landon.'

Arnold was also surprised. 'Mr Malling!'

'I hadn't realized archery was one of your interests.'

'Nor I yours.'

Tom Malling wrinkled his nose, and glanced down at his dog, standing close to his heels. 'I'm not in the slightest bit interested in archery. These people . . . overgrown children or subconscious psychopaths . . . I'm not sure which.' He frowned. 'I must confess to a certain curiosity, of course. The past . . . fascinates me. I think we have that in common.'

'Buildings, not weapons,' Arnold suggested.

'For me, people, and the way they behave,' Malling countered. 'I suppose it's one reason why I always come to the fete. One has to support charities, of course . . . but when people get together on occasions like this, something odd seems to happen. They behave in ways that are uncharacteristic.'

'I think I know what you mean,' Arnold replied, as he watched a stout lady, red in the face, trundling along in a three-legged race some fifty yards distant.

'Displays such as this bother me,' Malling said.

'I beg your pardon?' Arnold was confused.

'The archery. In other centuries, weapons such as the bow were used for war. This is different. It's an enthusiasm which borders on the unhealthy.'

'Why?'

'You can cause suffering with such weapons — even when they are of such modern manufacture. And that modernity, all this paraphernalia with these modern bows, it's as though it's caused by an obsession with death. In the old days things were different. Men tried to better their lot, control the evils that lurked among them, used weapons for functional purposes.'

'I think they still had archery meetings,' Arnold suggested, 'even in the fifteenth century.'

'Yes, to sharpen their skills! But not to play at death-dealing. Not to use weapons as instruments of mere pleasure. No, it was a simpler society, one in which standards of behaviour were measured more carefully, and in which justice and punishment — though hardly administered — were not befogged by changing social attitudes and weakness, liberal viewpoints, and a social conscience. Everyone knew his place; they all knew what the punishment might be for transgression; and there were groups of men who were empowered to order society.'

The conversation bothered Arnold: Malling's voice had taken on a disturbing intensity. Arnold was not quite sure what the farmer was talking about and in an endeavour to avoid the embarrassment he was beginning to feel, he made things worse. 'In any case,' he said, 'it seems the world and his wife is here at Long Meadow.'

The short silence that fell between them was sharp. Arnold was aware of the rising colour in his face and he looked down at his feet. 'I'm sorry . . . I seem to . . .'

'Just what exactly are you doing here, Mr Landon?' Malling asked in a cool tone.

Arnold shrugged. 'Wild goose chase, I suppose. I needed to see a man called Francis. Lives in Station Cottage. Or did.'

'*Did?*'

'I met his wife. She was leaving. It seems Mr Francis has . . . has left her.'

'I see.' The words lingered in the air between them, almost like portents. Arnold glanced at Malling's face: the farmer's features were calm but something raged briefly in his eyes, perhaps a memory of disaster or of loss. The passion was abruptly replaced by coldness as Malling met Arnold's glance, then turned his head, looking around them at the scattering in Long Meadow.

'I think, Mr Landon, I might be able to help you. You say you want to meet Mr Francis. I think that'll be him, just over there.'

The coldness in Malling's tone was marked with contempt and dislike. It found some echoes in Arnold's own feelings. Malling was pointing out the man with the grey-flecked beard who had been boasting of his successful slaughters in Kenya.

2

The man who was pursuing a legal action against Patrick Yates of Kilgour House was an individual very much in control of himself. He had a studied elegance which suggested he was aware of the attention he drew and battened upon it, encouraged it and honed it to his own advantage. His eyes were grey and crinkled in a friendly fashion as he spoke even though it was affectation that drew the veil of friendliness: there would be calculations behind the eyes that would not be for publication.

He was about forty years of age. He had spoken of his time in Africa. He must have been there for a number of years, since the mahogany of his skin owed little to the English sun. He had a wide mouth that hinted at a generosity Arnold guessed was spurious: there was something about the man that suggested he would always have an eye to the main chance, whether it was a business opportunity or a personal relationship.

As Arnold approached, the group he had been talking to was breaking up. Francis turned, became aware of Arnold's purposeful approach and half smiled.

'Mr Francis?' Arnold inquired.

'I am he.'

'My name's Landon.'

'I'm pleased to meet you.'

'I went up to Station Cottage but you weren't there.'

'No.' The grey eyes had hardened perceptibly, but the mouth still held the hint of a professional smile. 'I'm here. And you're looking for me, I presume. Are you a bill collector, Mr Landon?'

'Hardly that,' Arnold replied, shaking his head. 'I'm from the planning department at Morpeth.'

'I see.' Francis considered the information for a moment, while the smile faded. 'And what is it you want of me?'

'Well, we got your letter . . . I'm assigned to deal with the planning application from Patrick Yates, and I really wanted to talk to you, explain that our duties—'

'I'm not terribly concerned about your *duties*, Mr Landon,' Francis interrupted in a cold voice. 'I'm more concerned about my rights.'

'I understand that, but I'd like to explain our position to you.'

'And just what might that position be?' Francis drawled mockingly.

Arnold hesitated. 'The application from Mr Yates, it's one that we're called on to process. Now, of course, we have no legal interest in the dispute that you have with Mr Yates, and clearly we would have no argument to raise one way or the other—'

'But if you deal with the application,' Francis cut in, 'you would, in my view, be making a statement.'

'Surely, not so—'

'The statement being that you believe Mr Yates is entitled to undertake developments on the land in question. But I contend he has no such rights. I contend that he obtained that land by fraud, by undue influence, and by chicanery of the worst kind. And anyone who supports his situation in any way whatsoever is likely to find himself involved in the same kind of legal action I'm bringing against Yates!' His voice had risen, the heat in his blood reflected in a growing anger as he dwelled on real or imagined injustices. 'The fact is, Landon,

Yates has tried to cheat me out of my inheritance. I don't intend standing around to let it happen. I'd see the bastard dead first. But I warn you, I'm suing Yates, and if you step across my path I'll drag your bloody council in as well. And that, I believe, must conclude our conversation.'

'Mr Francis, please—'

'We've nothing more to say to each other, my friend,' Francis hissed, and the cold menace in his tone caused Arnold to withdraw the restraining hand he had held out in protest. He stood there, watching Francis march angrily away across the field towards the marquee, and after a moment, feeling humiliated and angry at Francis's rude dismissal, he turned away to head back towards the entrance.

The girl he had noticed earlier was standing some twenty feet away, staring at him. She seemed troubled, and as Arnold walked past her she stepped forward. 'Excuse me . . .'

'Yes?'

She hesitated. She suddenly seemed younger than he had thought, uncertainty removing the jauntiness in her manner, and she smoothed the leather guard on her arm in a nervous reaction that belied her previously confident air. 'You were talking to Bob . . . He seemed upset.'

'He was certainly rude.'

'He can be that.'

'Yes, well, if you'll excuse me—'

'Please, a moment . . . What was he upset about?' Arnold looked at her, took in again the short, attractively cut dark hair, and noted the squarish jaw that removed some of the femininity from her face, giving it a slightly masculine, over-positive look, and hesitated. 'I'm not sure I can tell you. It's his business . . . his reasons . . .'

'Not if it was about me,' she flashed.

Arnold observed her again, with curiosity. She seemed suddenly nervous and very vulnerable. 'I can't see what it has to do with you. I'm a planning officer, Miss . . . ?'

'Gregory,' she supplied. 'Wendy Gregory. I . . . I'm a PE teacher over at Broadwood,' she added inconsequentially. 'A planning officer . . . I thought . . .' She did not explain what she thought but stared wordlessly for a few moments at Arnold.

'Yes, well, it was a pleasure to meet you,' Arnold said after the awkward silence, 'but I assure you, it was a planning matter and—'

'It's about Kilgour, then.'

Arnold shook his head helplessly, unwilling to discuss the matter.

'Why don't you help him?' she asked with a sudden passion. 'Why do you make things difficult? He's in the right, you know!'

'Miss Gregory, I'm in no position—'

'The trouble is, Yates is a magistrate, a wealthy man even if it is Bob's money and land he's wealthy with — and it's always the same story isn't it? The Establishment, the clique, the society a man moves in, it'll serve to protect him. They all gang up on the outsider, the man who doesn't have the passwords, the *entrée*, the man who doesn't fit because his background isn't a cultivated one in the English scene! Oh, how I hate the *Establishment*!'

'Miss Gregory, I really don't know what you're talking about.'

'Then it's about time someone put you straight!' Miss Gregory's chin was set squarely as she glared at Arnold, determined to get her point across to him. 'I don't know how much you know about the background to the quarrel between Yates and Bob Francis, but believe me, it's not of Bob's making. All he wants — all he's ever wanted — is that which is his by right.'

'Miss Gregory—'

'I've no doubt the council at Morpeth will have heard one side of the story from Yates,' she sneered. 'After all, as a magistrate and an important figure in the county he'll have more than a few friends in the Establishment, Lord Lieutenant and all that jazz. But let's get at the facts!'

'I've already had a conversation with Mr Yates where he explained to me . . .'

'There you are!' Wendy Gregory exclaimed triumphantly. 'He's explained things, so that's all there is to it! But it's not the truth don't you see? Yates has twisted and perverted the truth to suit himself. He's well practised at it because he's been doing it for twenty years!'

An altercation seemed to have started near the marquee. An argument had developed, someone shouting angrily and waving his arms about, surrounded by a small knot of people. For a few moments Arnold hoped that the determined Miss Gregory might be sidetracked by the noise but she had her pale blue eyes fixed on Arnold and was not to be distracted.

'He'll have told you how he came to Kilgour donkey's years ago and helped Charles Edridge turn the estate around. But did he happen to mention that he was a solicitor who had been struck off?'

Arnold hesitated. 'No, he didn't mention that.'

'I should think not! Because it has a bearing on the whole story. It explains so much, you see: the truth is that Yates was removed from the roll of solicitors twenty years ago, shortly after he qualified, in fact, because of falsifications in the client's accounts of his firm. I don't know the whole story but Bob dredged it out — it seems Yates had ideas above his station even in those days and wanted to cut a dash — live beyond his means. He got his sticky fingers in the till, got caught, but the firm didn't prosecute. They didn't want to have the scandal, and I guess they weren't too happy to have their own negligent supervision exposed, so they were satisfied with his being struck off. That's when he first came into contact with Charles Edridge.'

Arnold took a deep breath. 'Miss Gregory, I really must interrupt. I'm a planning officer. I wanted to see Mr Francis because he has written to us, threatening to draw us into his lawsuit. He has refused to discuss the matter and I don't see therefore that what you tell me is relevant—'

'If you listen, you'll understand!' Wendy Gregory flashed at him. 'It's because people haven't been prepared to listen that that bastard Yates has got away with things for so long!'

The noise at the marquee had risen, the argument spilling inside the tent, with someone running across towards the cars parked at the far end of the Long Meadow. Arnold's attention was dragged back to the insistent Miss Gregory.

'He wheedled his way into Charles Edridge's affections. Yes, I use the word advisedly: *affections*. Oh, it wouldn't have started like that, of course. A good companion, a pleasant guy to have around at house parties. But the fact is, Charles Edridge was a funny kind of bloke. My own theory is that he was repressed as a child: dominant mother and all that. He went to Cambridge, grew up trying to be one of the smart set, went out to Kenya with his cousin, Bob's father, did a bit of farming there, but somehow, something was *wrong*. Bob's got some photographs taken on the French Riviera, the wealthy, smart set. Colonel Edridge is there, but standing so self-consciously, *pretending* to have a good time!'

Arnold eyed the angry young woman facing him. 'I'm not sure what you're trying to say,' he remarked, interested now in spite of himself.

'Look at those photographs and you'll see what I mean. He was *lonely*. He was in his late twenties, but he hadn't grown up. Maternally repressed, eager to show his manhood, wanting to be one of the boys, whatever the reasons deep down, in my view — and Bob's — basically he was a lonely unhappy man whose greatest problem was suppressed homosexual tendencies.'

'Are you saying . . .'

'Later events prove it,' Wendy Gregory said soberly. 'The guy was a closet gay. He didn't know it, or like it, and in those days it was a criminal situation to be in. But however hard he tried, in the end he had to admit he was homosexual.'

'Mr Yates told me that Colonel Edridge had married.'

Wendy Gregory made a humphing noise of contempt. 'What does that prove? He married a Swedish woman, but clearly she was unable to provide him with the security and affection he needed. The marriage failed, inevitably, because he was trying to live up to an image. And then Patrick Yates came on the scene.'

Arnold thought back to his visit to Kilgour House and his meeting with its owner. He shook his head. 'If you're trying to suggest that Yates . . . I have to say, there are some letters on the planning application file that would argue that Yates's inclinations are far from homosexual.'

Wendy Gregory smiled — a humourless smile that gave her features an unpleasant cast. 'You don't understand much about men and women, Mr Landon. I thought I made it clear that Patrick Yates has one objective in life: to better himself, make himself rich, *get on*. And he's ruthless as hell: he'd do anything to get what he wanted. He cultivated Edridge, became his friend, made himself useful in managing the estate, but he did more than that. He became Edridge's lover. And don't look so pained. The fact is, I'm convinced Yates is bisexual: I *know* he can get turned on by a woman. There was one occasion—' a slow flush of anger mixed with embarrassment stained her cheek. 'Well, no matter . . . but I'm telling you he's got quite a reputation in the county. There've been quite a few women who've fallen for his smooth charms — and who've been turned on by the insulting way he can treat a woman occasionally. More than one has got serious — there's been at least one divorce, and if rumour is true, there's even been a gas-oven case. But that's been his *fun*, and his real inclination: using women for sexual enjoyment. But that never stopped him from developing the relationship with Charles Edridge that he did.'

'But why?'

'To make Edridge dependent upon him, bind him closer, *commit* him,' Wendy Gregory said calmly. 'What can be said by way of pillow talk is more likely to be taken to heart than a conversation in the morning room over sherry before lunch.'

The anger seemed to have subsided at the marquee. The knot of people had broken up. Arnold caught a glimpse of Alan Evesham marching back to the tent from the line of cars. His stiff-legged walk suggested his customary ill humour had worsened and he was keen to vent his spleen on someone. Arnold was grateful suddenly that Wendy Gregory had detained him.

'This is all very interesting, Miss Gregory, but I still don't see what bearing it has upon my own interest in the situation.'

'I'm trying to fill you in on the kind of man Yates *is*,' she insisted, 'so that all you people at Morpeth don't get the wrong idea about Bob Francis. He's been wronged, you see, and yet he doesn't seem to be able to get the message across to the people who matter.'

'I can't say *I* matter,' Arnold offered feebly, but escape was not that easy.

'You're *involved*, and it's important you know and *understand*. When Bob was small, he remembers, Colonel Edridge was a frequent visitor: he spent summers with Bob's father. But everything changed after Patrick Yates came on the scene. It soured. Yates began to extend his influence over Edridge: made himself indispensable around the estate first, and then began to pour the poison into the Colonel's ear. There is no doubt that Bob was always regarded as Charles Edridge's heir, but Yates changed that, quite simply, by causing Edridge to believe that Bob was unworthy, and by *arranging* things in such a way that it seemed Bob's father was an enemy, rather than a friend.'

'Arranging things?'

Wendy Gregory smiled cynically. 'The short period Patrick Yates spent in the legal profession wasn't wasted. As I understand it from Bob, the estate needed a capital injection. There was a family trust of some kind, in which the capital was locked up. The Colonel couldn't touch it, but it seems Yates came up with the idea of breaking the trust, with the co-operation of Bob's father. The idea was that Colonel Edridge would actually draw upon the invested funds — there was a complaisant elderly trustee in the thing somewhere — and then Bob's father would bring an action against the trustee for breach. The idea was to get the thing formally aired, with a settlement being reached, a compromise being made out of court with a sum being handed over to Bob's father and the Colonel getting what he needed to sort out his problems financially.'

'But that's not what happened?' Arnold asked, intrigued.

'Exactly. The action came on, but somehow it wasn't the way it had been planned. It suddenly became serious. The lawyers weren't playing the game. The breach was being pursued. Bob's father couldn't understand it, but suddenly all communication between him and the Colonel ceased, no compromise was reached, he found himself as an aggrieved plaintiff — and he won.'

'I don't understand.'

'Neither did he. I mean, all Bob's father got out of it was a declaration. The trustee was found in breach of trust. There were costs of fifteen thousand quid, and the Colonel had to pay up. You'd have thought that would have damned Yates in Edridge's eyes, but the reverse happened. It was Bob's father who got cast as the grasping villain of the piece — and Patrick Yates as the supportive confidant of the Colonel. The whole business caused a serious rift in the family, and bound Yates even more closely to the Colonel — who was now getting on a bit and needing Yates more than ever. It was a nasty business altogether — and Bob firmly believes it was all clearly planned, right from step one.'

The story had the sad ring of truth to Arnold. It was plausible enough, given the possible nature of Charles Edridge. An isolated and distant man who had thrown himself into the social whirl of the upper set after university, in a desperate attempt to find a place for himself and his personality; a man perhaps with no great gift for friendship who had married to nullify the intensity of his dangerous sexual needs. After the break-up of the marriage, the clear impossibility of producing an heir could well have pushed Edridge towards a close relationship with his cousin, with the idea and intention that the son, Robert Francis, would eventually succeed to the Kilgour Estates.

But had Patrick Yates really played Iago in real life? Had he manoeuvred Edridge and Francis in an elaborate chess game where he would be the only eventual winner? And had the present owner in fact possessed the cold commitment to use sexual activity with Edridge to cement the relationship and eventually lay claim to the estates?

'No one in the family ever got to see Charles Edridge towards the end, you know,' Wendy Gregory asserted. 'He was kept locked away. There are stories in the village about the filthy rooms on the top storey where he lived, but that could just be malicious village gossip.' Wendy Gregory screwed up her pale blue eyes in thought. 'Difficult to determine, isn't it, between gossip and fact? But what I've told you is largely true. And it is true that no one saw Edridge for two years before he died. And the will left everything to Yates.'

'When did Mr Francis find out?' Arnold asked.

The woman shrugged, glanced around the meadow as though seeking confirmation from the man they spoke of. 'I'm not really sure. Several years, I'd guess. And Bob had adopted a . . . different lifestyle. He'd stayed on in Africa, got into safaris, that sort of thing.' She grinned nervously. 'I think he saw himself as a cross between Hemingway and Clark Gable in *Mogambo*, if you know what I mean. He was trying to write, got a few things published, but was out in the bush a lot. Bit isolated. Anyway, when he did get to hear about the estates, well, it was all a bit late. He was short of cash too, and . . . I understand there were problems with his wife . . . The upshot is, he was delayed returning, and when he did get back to England the lawyers told him it was all signed, sealed and difficult to upset. So, he took advice, moved into the cottage near here, got his thing together and took Yates to court. The law, of course, takes a hell of a time to get rolling. But it's finally on, at last.'

Arnold stared at the young woman. He nodded. 'I can understand all that. But why Mr Francis should want to drag us in . . .'

'He's touchy. You've got to understand,' she pleaded, 'he's had a rough time. He's become obsessed, the thing against Yates rules his head, he can't think of much else.

Maybe he . . . overreacts when he feels himself threatened, and the application that you're dealing with, well, it's another nail to shore up Yates's rights to the estate, you know what I mean?'

Arnold regarded Wendy Gregory carefully. 'And how do you feel about Mr Yates?'

She met his gaze boldly. 'He needs burying. The one satisfaction I have is what I once told him to his face. It was at the hunt ball. I was sixteen — just bloody sixteen, for God's sake, and he tried his charm on me. I laughed in his face. Then he tried to get a bit physical and I told him what I thought of him — old enough to be my father and coming on to me. Like I said: the man needs *burying*.'

'I get the impression that . . . feeling is heightened by the way you feel Mr Francis has been treated.'

The pale blue eyes slipped away momentarily. Then her chin came up. 'You could say that. I think Bob deserves to nail that bastard Yates, and I hope he does. If I can help, I will.'

'Like talking to me?'

'It may help.'

'Mr Francis has your full support, then?'

For a moment she seemed about to say something and then her glance clouded, as though she detected something behind the question that she was unwilling to deal with or admit. She stared at Arnold for a moment, and then without another word she turned and strode away, her muscular calves firm and strong, the line of her body stiff with something that could have been pride, or indignation, or determination.

Arnold would never know. But as he watched her walk away across the Long Meadow, stripping the leather guard from her arm, he wondered just how full her support for Bob Francis might be, and how far she would go in her furthering of his cause. It had led her to insisting that Arnold Landon have a full briefing of the story according to Bob Francis, merely on the basis that it might help Francis to have the planning office at least apprised of the 'facts', if that was what they were.

What was certain was that Francis was clearly capable of arousing a fierce loyalty in the breast of the young physical education teacher striding across the meadow. A loyalty that was in sharp contrast to the other image Arnold held in his mind: a woman in a raincoat, fading, disappointed and bitter, anxious to shed the last remnants of a relationship that had gone sour, and determined that the man who had left her should get nothing more from her as long as he lived.

CHAPTER FOUR

1

The following week remained hot and dry. Arnold spent the days working on some planning schedules that had been called for by the council, and his evenings tending his garden. At the weekend he drove out to Langton Castle, alone, and pottered around the ruin that Evesham had identified as the castle chapel. The glimmerings of some theories began to emerge in Arnold's mind, but the evidence was scant or even non-existent: and Arnold was aware of the dangers inherent in any such investigation, where enthusiasm for an idea caused the theorist to make facts fit those theories. He needed to do some reading, and more groundwork.

He found little time to dwell upon the planning application relating to Kilgour House. It was fairly straightforward, of course, apart from the objections, and he had arranged to meet several objectors in his office the following week. He did not set great store by the meeting: he had the feeling it would be unhelpful and difficult, because as far as he could see from the submissions they had little relevance to the planning application itself.

As for the character and lifestyle of Patrick Yates, that was none of his business. He admitted to being somewhat intrigued by Wendy Gregory's story, intrigued enough, indeed, to make some personal and discreet inquiries about Yates. He found responders wary. Yates had been elevated to the bench some years before and was reckoned a conscientious magistrate: the trouble was, it seemed, he was so conscientious that he sometimes went a bit over the top with some offences. Comments had appeared in the local press, suggesting that there were some people who seemed to want to make poaching a hanging offence, and one or two remarks had been made about Yates's sexual vitality, but Arnold had been disinclined to pursue them. Gossip of that kind was distasteful. Nevertheless, he did ponder upon the very real impact Patrick Yates seemed to make upon the women with whom he came into contact. His housekeeper, Pauline Callington, for instance: she had been a mixture of emotions, chief among which, Arnold suspected, was a cold rage that she had been treated as a servant by Yates in front of a stranger, when she clearly felt she deserved something better. A closer relationship, perhaps, than was normal, Arnold considered.

And then there was Wendy Gregory. There was no doubt she was in love with Bob Francis, and it was likely she was the cause of Francis leaving his wife. Idly, Arnold wondered whether Francis was now living with the physical education teacher with the pale blue eyes, though it was really none of his business. But gossip would be seething in the village, he had no doubt. As for her stories about the sexual predilections of the owner of Kilgour, well, Arnold was inclined to discount them. A sixteen-year-old girl could imagine things, and such memories would become enhanced by the passage of time, while other stories she had related or suggested seemed to Arnold to be the product of an overheated imagination, further fired by the breath of passion for Yates's enemy, Bob Francis. A bisexual who had led a woman to kill herself for love? It seemed unlikely to Arnold, not in this modern world. The older romantic years he himself dreamed of, well, perhaps it would have been different then . . .

Alan Evesham did not ring him during the week, to fix another appointment, but that did not disturb Arnold. The odd scene at Long Meadow when Evesham had clearly been upset about something had demonstrated to Arnold, even if he was not earlier aware of it, that the man had a nasty temper that could explode if he was crossed. Arnold felt that if new theories came to light about the chapel at Langton Castle it was quite on the cards that Evesham would explode again, and Arnold was not keen to be around in that event.

Nevertheless, he pottered around at the site, inspecting the greenish-yellow tiles in the wall more closely and making an effort to trace accurately the line of the walls. The building was certainly larger than would normally have been expected of a castle chapel, and there were internal wall foundations that suggested to him a more complicated set of inner cells than would have been normal. Time and again, however, his mind drifted back to the bricks above the Roman tiles. He could not be certain, but there was something odd about their colour, something he could not quite place. The doubt niggled at him, teasing him, and became oddly overlaid by the remarks Tom Malling had made to him about freemasonry, and the older, secret gilds of the masons.

Once again, the elusive butterfly of thought alighted in his brain, a comment Malling had made, a name he had mentioned . . . This time, before the mental insect could take wing again Arnold had seized it, the name at least: Richard atte Chirche.

He could not recall the context in which it had been used. But it was of little importance anyway.

* * *

On the Monday morning the three men filed into his office to discuss the objections they had raised in respect of the Kilgour planning application. Arnold had suspected it was going to be a difficult meeting and had fortified himself with an early cup of coffee. They sat ranged before him, two elderly men dressed in faded jackets and trousers, a second-best finery that had seen better days, and a younger man, stocky, clad in a checked shirt that strained against his deep chest, jeans and smart leather boots. There was something familiar about him, but Arnold had no time to dwell upon it as introductions were furnished.

'I'm Saul Eldon,' the man with the bald head and sad eyes announced. 'I farm on the Kilgour Estate — Ash Farm.' He contemplated Arnold for several seconds, his hound's eyes gloomy, his lower lip drooping as though all his life he had suffered disappointment, and then he said, 'It was Mr Francis who told us it was best we came personally to talk to you about the estates and the application and all that. This is Mr Norwich . . .'

'Sam Norwich.' This man was different. He had allowed Eldon to take the lead as the oldest of the three but devils of anger danced in his eyes and his brown gnarled hands were clenched, not from nervousness, but from a barely controlled temper. It was not his present surroundings that bothered him, but what he saw as the injustices of years. He wanted action. He made Arnold nervous.

Arnold looked at the young man with the black curly hair. 'I'm Nick Enwright,' the man said, and Arnold recalled where he had seen him: at Long Meadow, drawing the bow of laminated graphite. The man's face was hard, his mouth set: he would be regarding this meeting as a waste of time. For him there would be other ways in which to solve a problem, and they wouldn't involve talking. Arnold swallowed, and turned back to Saul Eldon.

'I'm the planning officer dealing with the application in which you have an interest and to which you've raised objections. My name is Landon. I'm afraid my unpleasant duty is to tell you that I can't see anything in your submissions which gives grounds for raising the objections you do. I mean, there are no legal infringements mentioned, no problems that can be put before the planning committee in due course—'

'Mr Landon, we want justice,' Saul Eldon pleaded. Nick Enwright stirred, annoyed at the pleading, but remained silent as Saul Eldon continued. 'I've been on the Kilgour Estates for over twenty years, Mr Landon. You need to listen to me. When the Colonel ran the place himself we had certain agreements and he always honoured them, because he was a gentleman. He maintained all the fences around the woods, and the windbreaks. He let us take fallen timber for firewood. He paid half the cost of repainting the windows and doors of the cottages—'

'For God's sake, Saul,' the angry man beside him interrupted, 'them days is long gone.'

'Even so, Sam,' Eldon insisted wearily, 'it has to be said.'

'Things changed when Mr Yates took over the management of the farms,' Sam Norwich argued, his eyes narrowed angrily as he made his point. 'You've been out there, I believe. You've seen how some of the farms and cottages have been allowed to rot — and we know why. So that Yates can get more money after the tenants have gone. And he can raise more money on the vacant property, for himself.'

'I'm afraid there's nothing illegal in that,' Arnold suggested. 'And no breach of the planning regulations—'

'Just hold on there,' Norwich interrupted, almost spitting out the words. 'I could tell you about the way he treated the Beverlys. They came in on Bolton Farm, rebuilt part of the house, redecorated, farmed the land, and they had three hundred good acres, dairy and arable. They worked their guts out. But Yates stopped paying for capital improvements, there were some bad years, the rents went up, the Beverlys couldn't pay and the bastard made them bankrupt so they had to leave the farm. Mrs Beverly does domestic work now up at Broadwood. It ain't right, Mr Landon, so don't talk to us about legal things!'

'But I have to. My powers are related to planning law—'

'*Planning!*' Norwich snorted indignantly. 'Tell him, Saul. Tell him what fix planning's got you into!'

Saul Eldon scratched his bald pate reflectively and sadly. 'The roof of the house is leaking, but Mr Yates, he won't get it repaired. The rent's gone up, but there's been no improvements made for years. Then the inspector from the Health and Safety Executive, he came around. I don't know who called him in—'

'*Yates!*'

'—and he told me I wasn't to enter the Long Barn because it was too dangerous.'

'He did the same down with me,' Norwich said. 'There's three cottages on Back Field Farm, which is my holding. Only one can be lived in. I got a man there and he says it's squalid. He's leaving me. One of my barns was actually demolished after the inspector came around. He wouldn't even go inside: stood back and said it was too bloody dangerous.'

'And what about your other barn?' Nick Enwright interrupted, leaning forward, upper arm muscles rippling under his shirt. 'That bugger got burned down. You going to say it was an accident?'

Norwich glowered at the younger man. 'I don't know. It's still a useless shell, that I know, even though Yates got the insurance money two years ago.'

'The point is, Mr Landon,' Saul Eldon said, 'what's to be done to stop the bleeding away of the estate? Mr Yates has put in this planning application. It's all for improvements on the farms under his own control. But the tenancies, they're a different matter. Over the past twenty years, ever since Mr Yates got involved at Kilgour, things have gone from bad to worse. Tenants have been leaving steadily. When Mr Yates came, there was fourteen farms tenanted at Kilgour. You know how many are tenanted now?'

'*Seven,*' Nick Enwright growled.

'And two of those is farmed by me,' Norwich added, 'and one other is nothing but a smallholding, if truth be said.'

'It's a desperate situation, Mr Landon.' Saul Eldon scratched at his bewildered pate. 'We don't know what to do. We've tried talking to Mr Yates. The Colonel now, he'd listen, discuss things. Mr Yates won't even talk. Sends messages.'

Like the Senior Planning Officer, Arnold thought sadly. 'It seems to us it's wrong, like, that this application should go through, and Mr Yates should spend all this money on improvements around the big house, when there's so much needs to be done—'

'And should be done, legally,' Norwich interrupted.

'—around the tenanted farms. So we want to register objections, Mr Landon. We want Mr Yates's application turned down. We want him to accept his responsibilities under the tenancies.'

Arnold shook his head. 'Gentlemen, sadly, I don't think I can help you. As far as I can see from your written submissions, there has been no breach of the Agricultural Holdings Act 1948 and so there's nothing we can do. In all other respects, although your submissions would seem to suggest bad mismanagement of the estates, there's no grounds here for denying the application. Mr Yates is the legal owner. It's his income, his money to spend. He can spend it as he wishes, without reference to anyone. We can exercise planning control, but as far as I can see none of you is affected by the improvements: they are not detrimental to your properties or your enjoyment of them—'

'He should spend the money on the tenanted farms!' Sam Norwich almost shouted. 'But you ineffectual buggers here in County Hall will do nothing to stop him souring the land!'

'We have no power—'

'You have no guts, you mean!' Norwich stood up, clenching his fists. 'Come on, lads, we'll get no joy here. We'll have to sort this thing out for ourselves. I've always known it: it was a mistake coming to weak-kneed pussyfooters here in Morpeth! It's up to us. It's *always* been up to us.'

He turned and stalked towards the door, body rigid with anger. After a moment's hesitation Saul Eldon rose, more reluctantly, as though still hoping Arnold might have something positive to offer. Then he hurried out behind his fellow tenant-farmer.

Nick Enwright had risen too. He stood facing the desk behind which Arnold sat and he glared at Arnold as though aware of a violent course of action but not certain whether to pursue it. He wet his thick lips and tensed his fingers, as though itching to get them wrapped around the limb of a weapon of destruction, his powerful bow. 'I got a different problem, Mr Landon. Have you got a couple of minutes?'

Arnold contemplated the thick, strong fingers. He had a couple of minutes.

Enwright sat down again. He stared at his hands, as Arnold stared at him. He was in his late twenties. His hair was black and thick and curly, and there was a sensual softness about his mouth that seemed out of character. The young man was clearly concerned to develop a 'macho' image: his preening at the Long Meadow display had demonstrated that, but Arnold wondered how much of that was based on insecurity. Then Enwright looked up and Arnold changed his mind. The young man's mouth might be soft, but it meant indulgence and selfishness, not sensuality, at least not of the sexual kind. He had brown eyes but they were of a remarkable coldness: there was something metronomic in his gaze, as though he was counting for effect. The silence grew between them as Arnold waited, a cold finger of anxiety touching the nape of his neck. He did not like Nick Enwright: the man had the coldness of a coffin about him.

'My father, he's in his late sixties now,' Enwright said. 'I work on the farm for him — Top Farm. It used to be good, Top Farm, but it's like the others now, pretty run down. But it's all I got.'

The farm, Arnold thought, and the bow he had used at Long Meadow.

'We got problems like the others' Enwright continued, 'but I got a paper as well. Look at it.'

Arnold was unwilling to refuse the grubby document pushed across the desk towards him: he had no desire to displease the muscular young man facing him. It was an agreement: he read it quickly. Among other things it committed the estate to undertake repairs to the main walls and roofs of the farmhouse and buildings on notification by the tenant. Arnold looked up.

'Is it all right?' Enwright asked belligerently.

'It seems in order.'

'The bloody walls need repointing. There's beams and slates need replacing in the roof. The chimney stack is shored up and the whole house needs weatherproofing. I can't get Mr Yates to do anything.'

Arnold frowned. 'Your father holds the tenancy?'

'That's right.'

'Then if Mr Yates is in breach of this agreement, as you say he is, my advice to you is, get your father to obtain a compulsory repairs notice from the District Council. They'll do it for you, I'm sure. After that, Mr Yates will have to remedy the defects.'

Enwright stared at Arnold with cold, glittering eyes. His lips moved back over his teeth as though he was imitating a snarling animal, and Arnold wondered briefly whether the young man was actually trying to give that impression. Perhaps he lived in a fantasy world, in which he postured, gave demonstrations which he himself observed from a distance, in another self.

'Mr Yates . . . he's got a down on me.'

'A down?'

'He's a magistrate.'

Arnold nodded, confused, 'So I understand.'

'My old man, he wants to hand the tenancy over to me in a year or so. He's been to ask Mr Yates, but he got a dusty answer. It's not right.'

'Your father wants to retire?' Arnold asked.

'Soon as he knows I got the tenancy, he'll pack up, live in the cottage. I'll look after him, he knows that. I can do that, Mr Landon.'

Arnold gnawed at his lower lip. Nick Enwright's head had lowered, hunching between his shoulders. Perhaps he now saw himself as a bull, ready to charge its enemy. Arnold frowned: he was getting fanciful, observing this young man's body movements. 'The law states that a tenant on retirement who wants to transfer the tenancy to his son is entitled to do so.'

'Mr Yates has got to do it?'

'He is under an obligation to do so.'

'And he's got to do the repairs?'

'He's contractually committed to it.'

'Then I got the bastard.' Abruptly, Nick Enwright rose to his feet. He towered over Arnold and dropped his elbows close to his sides, causing his pectoral muscles to bunch under the tight checked shirt. His eyes were glowing now, their dark depths alive with a malicious triumph. 'I been before him, you see. He put the boot in then, and I know he don't like me and wants to stop me taking over that tenancy. But now I know he can't, I've got the bastard. I'll make him eat dirt, this time. I'll shove his head in it. And if he don't do as I say . . .'

There was nothing sensual about Enwright's mouth now. It had thinned, and he was smiling, but it was the smile of a hunter, careless of life, sniffing for blood. A sudden image of death crossed Arnold's mind, and he asked, 'What did you appear before Mr Yates for?'

The glow in Enwright's eyes died. His glance dropped, and he frowned. He shook his head. 'It was nothing . . . they couldn't really prove much. He fined me, even though I knew he wanted to do something worse. It was just a pheasant . . . and a couple of salmon.'

He gave a curious ducking motion of the head and leered suddenly, his nostrils widening as though he savoured a lost odour, perhaps blood in the long summer grass, and then he walked out of the office.

Arnold sat still for several minutes. He was sweating. He could not explain what it was that bothered him, but something about Nick Enwright made his skin crawl. He had clearly built the body he was so proud of. The muscles were prepared, honed to a sharp fitness, and from the light way he moved on his feet he would be balanced, athletic out in the open.

Poaching. Just a pheasant, and some salmon. On the bench Patrick Yates was known to be hard. He would certainly have wanted to get his hands on Enwright; if the charge had been more serious, he would have done so.

Perhaps next time . . . In the meanwhile, Yates would be vindictive enough to deny the tenancy to the man who had faced him in the magistrates' court.

Arnold rose and walked across to the window. He felt hot and sticky and for some indefinable reason his heart was still beating faster than normal, as though he was alarmed by something. Like the presence of danger, or of evil.

Arnold's office window overlooked the car park. He looked out. There was someone standing near the wall at the exit. For a moment Arnold did not recognize him.

The man was standing in a tight, fixed pose. His legs were braced, the muscles outlined rock-hard in the tight jeans. His left arm was extended rigidly, his head of dark curls twisted, sighting along the line of his extended arm. The right arm was bent, the right hand near his ear. The whole of the man's body was immobile, tense, rigid with a controlled power, as he played out a role, acted out a fantasy in his head.

A deadly fantasy, in which a multi-bladed broadhead arrow would be aimed at a target.

The head moved, the tension slackened and the man turned to look back to the building he had just left a few minutes earlier. Nick Enwright looked up at the windows. He was smiling, the same smile Arnold had observed earlier. He could not have been aware of Arnold's presence, watching, but he smiled up to the windows, hugging a secret, cruel satisfaction to himself.

Then he turned and walked away with a smooth, swift gait, and a long, athletic stride.

Arnold shivered and touched his neck. His skin was damp. Someone should tell Patrick Yates that there were some men you should not make enemies of.

2

The courtroom was low-ceilinged and through the mullioned windows the morning sunlight glittered, dancing with dust particles, reflecting off the polished surfaces of the recently renovated tables. It was the first time Arnold had been in this room: he was used to planning inquiries held in County Hall, but the purpose-built courtrooms on the Ponteland road out of Newcastle were unfamiliar locations as far as he was concerned. The courtroom was already beginning to fill up: Arnold took a seat, unobtrusively, near the back of the room and he was not surprised to recognize several of the people who entered after he had claimed his place. The two older men who had been to see him in his office entered shortly after he did and nodded to him. The bald-headed tenant of Ash Farm, Saul Eldon, managed a gloomy smile, though his mournful hound's eyes remained sadly despairing of justice. Devils still danced in his companion's eyes, however. Sam Norwich still seemed to be simmering on the edge of explosion, and Arnold wondered whether the farmer ever did really calm down. Maybe he lived in a state of constant anger, a furious adrenalin keeping him active and snappish. He scowled in Arnold's direction, acknowledging his presence but tendering no polite greeting. He sat down grumpily, hunching himself forward, staring at his knees with his gnarled hands clasped tightly together in front of him.

Other men came in, generally middle-aged, lean of cheek, with the kind of skins that suggested a life in the open. Arnold guessed they would all have some connection with the Kilgour Estates, and had come to hear what the ultimate destination of the property might be, in terms of ownership. Their faces betrayed no feelings: unlike Sam Norwich, they were not willing to demonstrate their views openly. Perhaps they were being canny; perhaps they thought they had too much to lose if Patrick Yates succeeded and he saw disappointment in their eyes.

The landowner himself came in surrounded by a little flurry of people: his solicitor, a man Arnold vaguely remembered from Morpeth; a barrister whom Arnold had seen on the circuit from time to time; two clerks dancing attendance on the fussy solicitor clutching a bundle of papers, and, rather surprisingly, Pauline Callington. Yates had described her as his housekeeper, a term she had clearly resented; it was interesting to note she seemed to hold a sufficiently important place in his household to be accorded the privilege of a seat beside him in a hearing of such importance to his future. She seemed softer of features than Arnold remembered, and although her mouth was set rather grimly as the surroundings perhaps demanded, her pale blue dress emphasized her figure discreetly and she showed a great deal more femininity than when she had snapped her eyes at Arnold that day in Kilgour House.

Wendy Gregory came in alone. She stood hesitantly in the doorway for several seconds, and there was an odd strained set about her mouth that betrayed her nervousness. Patrick Yates raised his head and stared at her. From where he sat, Arnold was able to catch a glimpse of the wolfish contempt in the man's glance as he stared at the woman. She was aware of Yates's scrutiny and a slow flush coloured her cheeks, but she did not look at him. She hurried along the line of seats and approached Arnold.

'Is there anyone sitting there?'

Arnold shook his head and gestured to the seat beside him. Wendy Gregory slid into it, the strain in her face slowly subsiding. She appeared not to recognize Arnold and he suspected she was preoccupied with other things than being pleasant to brief acquaintances in whom she had no interest.

Arnold cleared his throat. 'It's one of the peculiarities of the English language,' he suggested.

She stared at him, recognition arriving in her glance, late and uncertain. 'What is?'

Her normally pale eyes were dark and confused, the lids heavy, and Arnold wondered, briefly and uncharacteristically, whether she would look like this in the dimness, when Bob Francis made love to her. He struggled to clear his thoughts, rearrange them. 'You asking me if anyone's sitting on an empty seat. If it's empty, logically, no one can be sitting there.'

Her eyelids flickered in incomprehension. He tried again. 'It's the same if you asked whether the seat was taken.' He tried a smile. 'If it was taken, it wouldn't still be there would it?'

She withdrew slightly, as though he were infected with something contagious. 'I don't know what you're talking about.' Her tone was cold and edged with finality.

Arnold grimaced to himself. It was the same with jokes. Usually, he forgot the punchline, or delivered it at the wrong point of time. He was not born to be a comedian nor a lounge lizard, nor a salon habitué indulging in small talk and gossip.

Oddly, the thought quite cheered him up.

In any case, Wendy Gregory had forgotten his existence again. She had tensed. Bob Francis had entered the room preceded by the hawk-faced barrister who was representing him. Arnold wondered how Francis could have afforded him: maybe it was his wife's money, for lawyers rarely took cases on the basis that they'd get paid only if they succeeded. Like doctors, their clients got buried or hanged too often to breed confidence. Or maybe it was Wendy Gregory who would be supporting Francis financially. He had glanced at her at last, and her body stirred as though she had been touched, the glance relaxing her, brief though it had been and non-committal, merely checking on the fact of her presence.

There was an usher at the door. He was trying to close it but someone outside was resisting. The door was pushed open and a young man slipped into the room. He made no attempt to sit down, in spite of the flapping hands of the usher. He stood against the wall, arms folded over his muscular chest. It was Nick Enwright.

The usher gave up, and Patrick Yates turned his head. His glance locked with Enwright's. His eyes were cold and unflinching, careless of Enwright's confident dislike. Arnold shook his head slowly — the enmity between these two men was open, and carried across this room even when other tensions could have taken precedence. There was a stir in the courtroom as the usher called them to attention. The judge was entering, to take his seat.

The audience finally subsided, with a buzz.

* * *

The hawk-faced barrister was called Wynne-Thomas and he spoke with just a trace of a Welsh accent that had been largely ground out of him by ambition and elocution lessons. He was summarizing the main issues in a final plea to the judge, Mr Justice Sykes, who had a reputation for severity as sharp as his cheekbones.

'In effect,' Wynne-Thomas was winding up, 'the argument for my client, Mr Robert Francis, is this. He had had every expectation of inheriting the Kilgour Estates. He had been on close and intimate terms with the late Colonel Edridge. They had corresponded affectionately. But from the moment that Mr Yates moved on to the estates as, eventually, manager, that relationship was systematically undermined, to such an extent that a rift developed in the family.'

Mr Justice Sykes raised his angular head and fixed Wynne-Thomas with an icy stare, calculated to encourage the barrister to brevity. Unabashed, Wynne-Thomas ploughed on.

'It is not my intention to dwell on the manner in which Mr Yates has used the estates for his own benefit. It is not within my brief to show how he has systematically set out to take the best short-term financial advantage of them — even though that action might be motivated by the realization that he might be called upon in due course to account for the estates to my client. But it is the essence of Mr Francis's case that the destruction of the relationship between the deceased colonel and my client was part of a deliberate plot by Mr Yates to influence the Colonel. That influence took the form of innuendo, advising on legal actions, the pouring of verbal poison into the susceptible old man's ear, and finally, guiding the hand that wrote Colonel Edridge's last will and testament.'

The judge sighed, leaned forward and scratched something out on the notes prepared in front of him. 'Mr Wynne-Thomas, will you be much longer?'

'I am almost finished, my lord,' replied the barrister, unruffled. 'But I would once again direct your lordship's attention to the background surrounding the making of the will. Mr Yates was in a position of influence — close personal influence — and he gave Colonel Edridge legal advice. There was no opportunity for other, independent legal advice. The Colonel was bedridden. Access to him was all but impossible. Mr Yates and his employees — for it was he who hired and fired, not Colonel Edridge — barred the way. The clerk who came to the house to witness the will played no part in its drawing up. And that will gave sole ownership and control of the Kilgour Estates to Patrick Yates. This, my lord—'

'You are now getting to the point, I trust?' Sykes queried, scratching the side of his nose with a lean, bony finger on which the nail seemed to curve like a claw.

'This is the contention of my client. The making of the will was bad in law. Colonel Edridge was subject to extreme undue influence. That influence was exerted over a period of years to such an extent that, at the end of the time, the bedridden colonel had no opportunity — or will — to form an independent judgement. He had been taken advantage of. The will should be set aside. The properties in question should then be allowed to fall to their rightful owner under the proper law of succession as it applies to intestacy. We ask, your lordship, for justice for my client.'

Wynne-Thomas sat down abruptly. There was a brief stir in the courtroom. As Wendy Gregory clenched her fists beside him, Arnold watched Wynne-Thomas with mild interest. The speech contained elements of floridity but had been delivered in a flat monotone that seemed to lack passion or commitment. Arnold was left with the view that Wynne-Thomas had been doing what he was paid for, and no more. His heart had not seemed to be in the argument he had presented. Possibly it was the inhibiting presence of Sykes in front of him, and yet he had seemed to be largely unmoved by the judge's interruptions or impatience.

Wendy Gregory muttered something under her breath. 'Your indulgence—'

Counsel for Patrick Yates was rising, but a brief gesture from Mr Justice Yates stopped him halfway and he remained in a half-crouching position like a wounded crow trailing a black wing.

'No need, no need,' Mr Justice Sykes announced snappishly. He waved his bony finger dismissively and spread out the papers in front of him with a bad-tempered frown. 'There are occasions,' he said, 'when one is called upon to deal with matters of great moment in the courtroom. They can be stimulating occasions. This is not one of them.'

There was a quiet hiss of breath from the woman sitting beside Arnold.

'It seems to me,' the judge continued, 'the facts in this case are relatively simple. Colonel Edridge intended — some years ago — favouring Mr Francis with ownership by inheritance of the Kilgour Estates. He changed his mind. He left them to his friend and companion and estate manager, Mr

Yates. A holograph will was written — *in Colonel Edridge's own hand*. That will was witnessed, by an independent witness. That will was later proved. The person who benefited under the will took possession of the estates and used them — under his legal entitlement — as he wished. These are the facts.'

Wynne-Thomas was not looking at the judge. He was beginning to collect his papers. Barristers were busy men: they had many legal fish to fry.

'Facts are, of course, open to different interpretations. After all this happened, Mr Robert Francis emerged from whatever fastnesses had held him over the years to claim, somewhat tardily, what he regarded as his inheritance. But all had been done. All had been settled. The only course open to him, if he was to overturn the situation, was to question either the facts or the interpretation . . .' Mr Justice Sykes shook his bony head sadly. 'Where something is argued, where a situation is to be resiled from by the law, it is necessary that certain proofs emerge. The burden of proof, in such cases as this, is known as the balance of probability: it was incumbent upon Mr Francis to show that, on the balance of probability, undue influence had been exercised. *Allegations* have been made . . . but where have been the proofs?'

The judge scowled at the papers in front of him, then favoured the whole courtroom with the same expression. 'Irrelevant considerations have been cast before us: they have wasted our time. We are not here to adjudicate upon the nature of Mr Yates's husbandry of the estates. The legality of the will itself has been tested in probate; that legality has not been seriously questioned in the hearing before us. We have heard no evidence that Colonel Edridge was of feeble mind — merely that he had reclusive tendencies. If he chose to spend his time largely with one companion only — Mr Yates — that was his business. It is hardly evidence of feeble-mindedness.'

From the manner in which Wendy Gregory wriggled on the seat beside him Arnold concluded that this was one point on which she certainly disagreed with the judge.

'Equally, there has been no firm, hard evidence of undue influence. Mr Yates was not acting as a solicitor, whatever his background might be. He did not draw up the will. It was holograph, properly witnessed. Where is the evidence of sustained undue influence? There is none. Mr Francis makes the allegation. But Mr Francis displays no proofs. Cases of this kind always raise the bodily temperatures of the people concerned: this heat can affect the logical movement of the mind. I confess to having seen no merit in the plaintiff's case at any point during these proceedings, and I conclude the case lacks merit. The motion for the setting aside of the will is accordingly dismissed. Mr Yates might have a case to answer in another court higher than this, but that is not our business. In law, he has no case to answer.'

'*Stupid old man!*'

The words burst from Wendy Gregory in a spurt of uncontrollable anger. Arnold started in his seat. The people around him froze. The judge's head came up; it was not certain he had heard the words themselves, but he had obviously been aware of the emotion that had sent them echoing around the courtroom. He stared at Arnold for several seconds, his blurred old eyes glinting viciously like a snake about to strike, then his glance slipped to Wendy Gregory. His snake's tongue touched his bluish, dry lips. 'Young woman, was that you?'

Wendy Gregory sat still, tightly wound up in her own terror.

'You have something to say?' snarled Sykes. 'Or is it merely a case of emotional, misplaced loyalty?'

He allowed an unpleasant smile to touch his old mouth, pleased at the fear he had instilled into the courtroom, and then, after a pause, he rose and made his way from the bench, trailing an embarrassed silence behind him.

When the door closed the courtroom broke into a confusion of sound as everyone tried to talk at once, to his neighbour, to his or her friend. Wendy Gregory remained silent. Bob Francis, seated at the front, was arguing vehemently with Wynne-Thomas who looked bored, shaking his head slowly, but positively. He stood up, and Arnold caught his words to Francis. 'I warned you, old boy, but you wouldn't take advice. I did my best . . .'

'He didn't,' Wendy Gregory muttered to herself. Her body was shaking with the release of tension. *'He didn't!* He wasn't even trying.'

But he had never believed in the case, Arnold considered. Maybe it was Wendy Gregory's money that was paying the legal bills. Or maybe she was simply upset because the verdict had gone so harshly against Bob Francis and in favour of the man she hated, Patrick Yates.

The small group around Yates was breaking up from a brief flurry of self-congratulation. Patrick Yates himself seemed cool enough, though there was an unnatural brightness about his eyes, and a slight, self-satisfied smile marked his mouth as he glanced across the room towards the plaintiff. Francis caught the glance and went pale. WynneThomas said something to him but, ignored, he shrugged and walked away. The crowd in the courtroom began to thin; Sam Norwich stumping grumpily away with a red face, suppressing his natural anger, Saul Eldon stoop-shouldering his way towards the doorway with his mouth down-turned and his glance on the floor. Arnold could not guess what they might have hoped for under the regime of Bob Francis: it might have been worse than they had bargained for, since there was nothing to suggest they would have fared better with a new owner. Francis was a globe-trotter who had come home only when money beckoned: he might have intended bleeding the estate in ways not dissimilar to Yates's. But the matter was hypothetical. They were stuck with Yates as their landlord.

Arnold began to make his way forward. At least his problems were largely resolved. With Francis defeated, there was nothing to prevent the smooth dealing with the planning application regarding Kilgour. The issues would be clear-cut: an application of planning law and practice, untrammelled by legal complications involving third parties, with or without *locus standi*.

He found himself unable to reach the door. Wendy Gregory and two or three other people barred the way. They stood, avid in their attitudes, listening to the exchanges that were arising between plaintiff and defendant.

'You're a damned fool,' Patrick Yates was sneering. 'You must have been advised right from the start that this action was a waste of time.'

Bob Francis stood facing him, his studied elegance now dissipated by the heat of his growing anger and disappointment. His mahogany skin had reddened, blood flushing in fury as he faced his enemy and the reality of his emotions was now displayed in the twist of his mouth, all hint of generosity gone as dislike and hatred for Patrick Yates scarred his features. 'You've cheated me, damn you, cheated me!'

Unlike Francis, Yates was in control of himself. He smiled cynically, holding his head erect, tilted slightly as he observed the younger man. 'Cheated? Not at all. You've cheated yourself. The fact is, Francis, you've been a damned fool in all of this. Had you come to me reasonably in the first place, everything might have been different.'

'Like hell it would!'

'I might have been persuaded of the justice of your case,' Yates drawled mockingly. 'I mean, out there in the bush . . . It was hardly your fault that you lost touch with Charles. You could certainly not be expected to behave in a familial way, at such a distance, with such problems of communication . . . I mean it's not reasonable, is it? And you weren't to know that Charles and I would become such close friends—'

'Too damned close, I hear!' Francis flashed.

Patrick Yates paused, still in control of himself but now cooler, more deliberate, a little of the mockery gone to be replaced with an edge of menace. 'And you weren't to know that Charles would forget you, ignore you . . .' As he shifted, turning slightly, Arnold caught a glimpse of Yates's house-keeper, Pauline Callington. She was standing at his elbow, watching Francis carefully. She put out a hand, touched Yates in a possessive, warning manner. Yates ignored her.

'But as I said, you're a damned fool. Always were. You should have come home years ago, fought for your inheritance then, looked after the old fool the way I did. And as for this action . . . it was always doomed to failure. Wynne-Thomas told you, right from the start. But who knows? If you'd come to me, pleaded with me, *begged* a little . . .'

The fury in Francis's features was naked now. Arnold was suddenly reminded that this man had lived in the bush, would know how to defend himself in the wild, and something of it showed in him now, in the menace of his mouth, the dangerous way in which he glared at Yates, leaning forward at the hips, almost as though he was ready to leap at the magistrate.

'If you think I'd ever beg from you, let alone from any-one . . .'

'But my dear boy, isn't that how you get by?' Yates inquired with a pleasant malice. Pauline Callington must have squeezed his arm suddenly, warningly, because he turned his head towards her for a moment, stared at her. He sneered. 'There are all sorts of people who beg in their own way. Women, particularly . . .'

Pauline Callington's glance hardened as she stared at Yates. Her hand dropped away, as though she had been stung by words meant as much for her as for Yates's main target.

'But from women,' Yates was continuing, 'one can expect it. One takes receipt of favours and expects to pay for them. But when a man—'

'Yates, I'll close your mouth. I'll close it for good!' Francis's mahogany skin was paling now, anger being replaced by the steel of determination.

'But surely I haven't got it wrong, have I?' Yates mocked him recklessly. 'I mean, as I understand it, you only married your wife for the money she had. And with that running out, and with the lawsuit here beckoning, you had to get cash elsewhere.' He paused, turned his head and slid a sly glance in the direction of Wendy Gregory. 'And you'll always find some stupid little slut who'll give all for love — and money as well!'

133

'Patrick . . .' Pauline Callington's tone was firm. She moved forward, slipping between him and Bob Francis. 'I think this has gone far enough. Time we went home.'

'My dear lady,' Yates soothed, 'if Francis can nurse his disappointment, surely I'm allowed to enjoy my victory?'

Wendy Gregory, standing in front of Arnold, was trembling violently. She was staring at Bob Francis, but he seemed unaware of her presence, unmoved even by the shaft Yates had aimed in her direction. He was beside himself with disappointment and fury, but his anger was channelled now, his whole body tense, like a predatory animal set to kill. Oddly, that tension gave him added control, and his mouth was like a piece of bent iron. He said nothing, glaring at Yates, and the magistrate, unmoved, sneered back. After a few moments Francis turned away and stalked out of the courtroom. Wendy Gregory was shaking. She put out her hand, swaying. Arnold caught her by the arm. 'Are you all right?'

She seemed unaware of him and yet she leaned heavily, dizzily against his restraining arm. He guided her to a seat. Mercifully, they were at the back of the group and no one seemed to notice as she sank into the chair. Yates and his entourage were making their triumphant way out of the room in the wake of Bob Francis. Wendy Gregory's fingers gripped Arnold's wrist. She took a deep breath, and the fingers tightened. He was reminded of her occupation: the teaching of physical education. She had strength and it was communicated to him as she gripped hard, seeking control. Her head turned, she stared at him, her eyelids blinking rapidly as though seeking for tears that should have come or were being forced back. 'Do I know you?'

'Arnold Landon. We met at the archery club meeting the other day.'

She nodded, half-remembering, then other memories, more recent, clouded her glance. She released his wrist quickly. 'I'll be all right.'

'Are you sure—'

'Thank you, I'll be all right. I was dizzy for a moment . . . the heat of the room . . .'

Arnold hesitated, then stood up, reluctant to interfere where his assistance was not required. Embarrassed, he mumbled, 'Well, if you're sure . . .'

'Quite sure,' she said in a quiet but firm voice, without looking up at him. Arnold nodded, and made his way slowly out through the doorway of the courtroom. When he glanced back she was still sitting there. She appeared to be crying.

The entrance to the courtroom lay at the top of a wide balustraded staircase. From the top of the stairs Arnold could look down the well to the ground floor. He paused, looking down: nearing the foot of the stairs was Yates, with Pauline Callington beside him.

Standing just inside the main doors was Nick Enwright.

In spite of himself Arnold stopped, and waited for the inevitable meeting. It was not curiosity so much as a reluctance to become involved in the scene that he guessed was about to occur. Patrick Yates had won his case and was in an elated frame of mind, but the young man waiting for him was clearly intent on disturbing that equanimity.

As Yates and the woman reached the bottom of the staircase Nick Enwright stepped forward.

'Mr Yates.'

The magistrate hesitated, then turned his head, muttered something to Pauline Callington.

'Mr Yates!'

Reluctantly Yates faced the young farmer. 'What do you want?' he asked curtly.

'You did well in there, *sir.*'

'What's that to do with you?'

'Nothing, like. Except it's good to see someone riding high before a fall.'

'What's that supposed to mean?'

Nick Enwright was grinning, unpleasantly. 'Just that you win some, you lose some.'

'You're talking in riddles, Enwright.'

'You won today, *sir.* But with my dad, well, it's going to be a different story.'

Yates paused, looked Enwright up and down contemptuously. 'Are you drunk?'

'Not at all. But I been taking advice.'

'Not before time,' Yates said curtly and tried to push past. Enwright barred his way. 'What the hell do you want?'

'I told you, I been taking advice. My old man's been hanging on at the farm tryin' to persuade you to let me have the tenancy so he can retire. *Now* I learn you can't do that, not in law you can't. There's an Act that says you got to hand over the tenancy to the son, if he wants it. My dad wants it, and I want it. He'll retire, I'll work the farm. And I'll do a bloody good job, Mr Yates, with or without your help. Believe it!'

Yates stared at the young man with open dislike. 'Enwright, you're a wastrel. You'd spend more time shooting game than you would in looking after the farm. There's no way I'll let you have that tenancy.'

'You can't stop it!'

'I can stop it,' Yates said viciously. 'I've got other plans for that farm — or at least for the capital I can raise with it in due course. As for your tenancy and your protected rights at law, you're misinformed, my friend. Yes, it's true the Act says the son is entitled to take on the tenancy after his father — but there's a proviso. It says *if he is suitable.* Are you *suitable,* Enwright? Do you think your claim would stand a cat in hell's chance against my word? Particularly when I can point out that you have a criminal record! Now get out of my way and stop bothering me, or I'll call the police on you!'

For one long moment Arnold thought Enwright was going to stand his ground. His muscles tensed and his fists were clenched. Then, swiftly, the tension died in him, he grinned wolfishly and stepped aside. Yates brushed past him, and Pauline Callington hurried behind. They walked through the open door and down the pathway to the main road.

They did not look back. If they had, they would have seen what Arnold observed. Nick Enwright stared after them for a few seconds, then suddenly he snapped into swift, polished movement, taking up precisely the same stance Arnold had seen him hold in the car park outside Arnold's office.

But this time, in his fantasy, the broad headed arrow was directed at a human target.

3

Early the following week Arnold was somewhat surprised to receive an invitation from Professor Agnew to attend a morning sherry party he was giving in his department at Newcastle University. When he thought it over Arnold concluded it was by way of a thank you for the work he had agreed to undertake with Professor Evesham, so he considered it would be churlish to refuse. He regarded himself as unsuited to the atmosphere of sherry parties — he preferred solitude on the wild hills — but he liked Agnew, so he decided to go.

When he entered the building the porter seemed to be reading the same newspaper he had been buried in the last time Arnold had visited the building. He did not look up as Arnold entered.

The room in which Professor Agnew was receiving his guests was located on the same floor as Evesham's workroom so Arnold knew more or less how to get there. He walked along the corridor until he came to Evesham's room; the door was open, and he hesitated at the entrance. The papers were scattered over the desk, and the display of arms was clearly visible, but there was no sign of Evesham himself. Feeling that he had escaped, Arnold hurried past and along the corridor to the elegant, tall-ceilinged room where Agnew was waiting. As he entered, Agnew came forward, smiling, a welcoming hand extended, and Arnold realized he had not escaped for, behind Agnew, at the edge of a small group of people, stood Alan Evesham, holding forth in some passion, waving his sherry glass to emphasize the points he was making.

'Mr Landon,' Agnew exclaimed. 'Delighted you could make it. The young lady will take your preference.' He beckoned to the nubile young secretary who was now doing duty as a sherry waitress. 'Dry, medium, sweet?'

'Medium, please.'

'Amontillado. Now then, introductions . . .'

There were several academics, a professor of engineering from Nottingham, two industrialists and the managing director of a shipping business on the Tyne. Two members of the boards of nationalized industries were introduced to him, along with a man from ICI, and Arnold was beginning to think he was in the wrong company and dazed with the rush of names and jobs and faces — most of which seemed to glaze over with lack of interest when they learned his occupation — when Agnew said, 'And of course, you know Tom Malling.'

The farmer shook Arnold's hand, and Agnew slipped away. Malling eyed Arnold for a few moments, then sipped ruefully at his glass. 'Not exactly my tipple.'

'Nor mine.'

'Prefer a straight Scotch myself.'

'I'm not a great drinker.'

'Well . . . I indulge a little too much, sometimes.' There was a reflective gleam in Malling's eyes for a few seconds, as though he considered loneliness and its solution, and then he shrugged and smiled vaguely. 'I'm not sure why I'm here, among this lot.'

'It's a feeling I've already had,' Arnold replied.

'What's your conclusion?'

Arnold looked around the room at the men in their business attire and the academics in their grey suits and considered the matter. 'I guess Professor Agnew is killing a couple of birds at the same time.'

'How do you mean?'

'The businessmen . . . he's out to strengthen his acquaintanceship with them. They like being called socially to the university. Flatters them. Academia is something they might aspire to later, when they've made enough money to afford it. Mastership of a college, that sort of thing.'

'We hardly fall into that category.'

'Ah no, but with us it's a matter of expressing gratitude in a discreet way. The academics here are present for a purpose, but we're makeweight, socially. Interesting, perhaps, as curiosities — a talking point later, over dinner. Not that Agnew would consciously do that.'

'No, he wouldn't.' Malling glanced around the room at their companions. 'I quite like old Agnew. That other fellow, though — Evesham — I dislike him. Rude sod.'

Arnold made no comment. After a while Malling looked at him thoughtfully and said, 'You and Evesham don't exactly see eye to eye either.'

'No?'

'He doesn't care for your involvement with his affairs. Up at Langton.'

'Is it that obvious?'

'He was like a bear with a sore backside.' Malling paused. 'But he's about to do the decent thing, it seems.'

Alan Evesham had broken away from the group he seemed to have been terrorizing with his erudition and his dangerously waving glass and was bearing down on Arnold and Tom Malling.

'Morning, gentlemen,' he said, unable even with such a greeting to avoid a hint of belligerence. 'Slumming, hey?'

There seemed little they could make by way of adequate reply. Evesham didn't need one. He clearly had imbibed several sherries, and his features were slightly flushed. He prodded Arnold in the chest with his forefinger, and a spot of sherry splashed on to Arnold's tie. 'You got any further with our friend?'

'Friend?'

'Bloody Ailnoth! Got no other friends in common, have we?'

Arnold wondered whether the boorish Professor Evesham could have any friends at all, but aloud he said, 'I'm afraid not. I've not really had time to—'

'Time, time, inclination more bloody likely! Can't guess why Agnew saddled me with you. I mean, what have you come up with?'

Arnold opened his mouth but the question had been rhetorical. Evesham continued, his eyes glittering with excitement and alcohol. 'Dammit, I'm certain Ailnoth is the guy buried up there at Langton, and if only Agnew would release the funds I could get on with my thesis and develop it properly. Not until some confirmation comes from you, he says. But I'm not turned on by gifted amateurs, Landon, you know that?'

'It hadn't escaped my attention,' Arnold replied bleakly. 'You've met Tom Malling, of course.'

'Yes, that's right, up at Langton Castle.' His eyes wandered around the room, and finally returned to his glass. 'You'll excuse me.' He walked away to replenish his glass, putting his arm around the flustered, unhappy secretary as she poured and taking the chance to whisper in her ear. She clearly disliked the experience.

Malling sighed. 'Not exactly the most sociable of men.' Arnold was forced to agree.

'Are you going to be able to support his Ailnoth obsession?' Malling asked. 'Have you discovered anything more?' When Arnold shook his head, Malling continued, 'And what about that chapel up at Langton? Have you had any further thoughts about that?'

Arnold hesitated. There was the puzzle about that chapel, but preoccupation with other things had caused him to thrust the problem to the back of his mind. He shrugged. 'I'll have to think more about it. There's something that puzzles me about it, the colour of the tiles, or maybe it's an association of ideas, I can't be sure. I just haven't had time . . .'

Malling nodded in sympathy. He was silent for a little while, both men glancing around the room, noting the way interest groups seemed to have congealed in various corners heads bobbing in earnest conversation. After a while, in a voice that seemed to struggle from him with difficulty Malling said, 'You'll have heard about . . . about Yates: and Kilgour House.'

'The lawsuit, you mean?'

That's right. Francis failed in his attempt to wrest Kilgour from that . . . that scoundrel Yates.'

'I was at the hearing. It seems Francis never really had a leg to stand on. Or so the judge seemed to think.'

Malling scowled, grimacing at his drink as though he found It suddenly distasteful. 'Six of one, though, isn't it?'

'How do you mean?'

'They are both . . . unpleasant men. *Scum.*'

The vehemence of the word seemed to shock Malling himself, even as he uttered it. Somewhat confused, he sipped his drink and shook his head. 'I mean, they're both arrogant men who are prepared to ride roughshod over the rights of other people, seize what they want out of life in spite of what it may cost their neighbours. Neither of them *deserved* to win that case. Both of them should be consigned to perdition. Maybe they will be one day.'

'I've yet to meet anyone who seems to have a good word to say for Yates,' Arnold muttered reluctantly. 'As for Francis, well, I can't say I know him particularly well. A fleeting conversation—'

'He's tarred with the same brush as Yates,' Malling interrupted passionately. 'The pity is, there's such a gap between law and justice. The two are not synonymous.'

'Were they ever?'

'They ordered these things better in the old days,' Malling mumbled.

'How do you mean?'

'The sworn masons—'

'Masons?' snapped the voice from just behind Arnold.

'You talking about masonry?' It was Alan Evesham, back with his glass topped up. 'Better be careful, my lad, ought to whisper in these hallowed halls if you have a go at the masons. Vested interests and all that.'

'We weren't actually discussing masons,' Arnold said stiffly. 'We were talking about the lawsuit involving Patrick Yates—'

'That bastard!' Evesham snarled, his face mottling with a swift anger. 'I heard he'd got away with it. Owner of Kilgour! Did I ever tell you about the dig and the way he—'

'You did.'

'I've often thought of ways of getting back at him,' Evesham brooded, his eyes hooding with malice. 'But when you get down to it, there's only one remedy for a bastard like that. Extermination.' He squinted at his glass, raised it to the light, then looked owlishly at Arnold. '*Extermination.* Treat him like the vermin he is.'

* * *

Looking back at the event a week later, Arnold still shuddered, not so much for himself as for Professor Agnew. Quite what the industrialists had thought when Evesham began to hold forth upon military history and emphasize the immoral role played in war by businessmen it was difficult to say. Agnew had tried to hush the man, but clearly Evesham was not used to protracted bouts of sherry-drinking and he would not be quietened. Arnold had shrunk into an embarrassed corner with Tom Malling, and it was not long before the farmer, introverted and silent, had offered his thanks and withdrawn. Arnold had followed him as soon as was decent, and as he walked past Evesham's room with its clutter he wondered whether the military historian would be sleeping it off there overnight. He certainly would not be fit to drive out to his cottage that afternoon.

Malling had questioned Arnold about Langton Castle and Arnold felt a little guilty that he had since done nothing to assist Evesham and Agnew in the way he had been asked. He wondered now whether Evesham stood any chance anyway of getting Agnew's support for the grant, after the way he had killed Agnew's party. Even so, his own curiosity had been whetted that day up at the old castle; the only problem was finding time to do anything about it. The workload he carried was heavy, there were two inquiries to prepare for and there was a heavy backlog of paperwork on his desk.

On the other hand, he was due for some leave.

He buckled down to clear his desk and deal with the demands building up there, and then, on the Friday, he left a note for the Senior Planning Officer, explaining he was taking a day's leave that was due to him. There was no point in seeking an interview and, as it happened, an assent came to him within the hour.

He took the day off the following Monday.

It was a bright day, high clouds scudding across the blue sky with a fresh wind blowing in from the coast as Arnold drove inland and made his way towards the village and Langton Castle. The roads were deserted and he was able to enjoy the hedgerows and the fields. He was at peace with himself, he had secreted a half-bottle of wine with some sandwiches in the back of the car and he was looking forward to a day alone in the hills.

He parked near the church and made the ascent of the hill. Above Cheviot a dark cloud threatened, but here at Langton the sun was bright, the grass shining, and he climbed above the ancient walls until he could sit with his back against the crag and gaze down on what had been described as the old chapel.

The sun was warm on the back of his neck. He ate his sandwiches, drank his wine and ruminated, on the past, his own childhood in the Yorkshire Dales, the ancient wildwood, the patches of shadow that crept across the green fields below him, the tramp of military feet on these hills since Roman times, and before.

His eyelids grew heavy and he dozed, but when he drifted back to the modern world he was still thinking about the crag and the chapel and the hill.

'Of course it's not a chapel,' he said aloud to himself. Nor was it of that he was now convinced. The line of the land was clear, if you just sat down and looked at it for long enough. Lady Glynne-Stuyvesant had a great deal to answer for with her amateurish meddling. Not so much for what she had done, but rather for the theories, half-baked and erroneous, that she had propagated.

The line of the crag had been the original line of the ancient castle wall. Forget its age, disregard the arguments, but concentrate upon the logic. Along that crag the ancients would have built an earthwork. Later, much later, there would have been erected wooden defences, but never to any great height, never of any consequence. The fall of the land and the steepness of the crag would have formed the defensive line itself.

And the chapel was no chapel. It had been on the outer perimeter of the ancient wall, a watchtower perhaps, a command post with an extensive view over the valley towards the dangerous northlands and the border, and back down beyond the valley where Kilgour House lay.

How old? Ancient. It was inevitable. Among that scrub and trees had once stood an old building, and it would have been built on again and again. But the likelihood would have been that the builders would never have dug deep, not after the first sound, rock-based foundations had been constructed for them. That would account for the old bricks. Why lift them from a solid foundation? Rather, reuse them and build upon them, century after century, until finally the castle lost its usefulness and the shepherds came in and broke down the walls for their own uses on the hills, and the scrub and the trees arrived, making their own insidious green shroud to hide the broken truth.

But there was something drifting in his mind, a piece of information he could not slot into place, even though it was only half-remembered, half-digested.

He rose to his feet to gather up the empty bottle and the wrapping paper, and stood on the crag, looking across the fields, frowning. Somewhere in the distance a dog was barking excitedly: he could see it racing across the field, streaking home as he watched, but he barely thought of it as he puzzled, trying to trap the elusive words that tumbled somewhere in his brain, clicking together, but never into place.

Finally, annoyed with himself, he walked back down from the crag, realizing that further struggling would only be counterproductive. Forget about it, and it might return.

It was probably unimportant anyway: better to enjoy the day. He still had nothing to help Evesham, but at least he was out in the clean air of Northumberland.

Arnold did not pause in the village. He returned to his car and decided to drive back the long way, through the winding lanes and across the dipping roads over the hills, south first, and then east back towards Morpeth.

It was when he rounded the bend about a mile from the village that he saw the car in the ditch. The woman was standing helplessly near the offside wheel. It was Pauline Callington.

She was stiff, rather formal, and was unwilling to be grateful, but yes, she was in trouble. It would seem that something had gone wrong with the steering. She'd been shopping, was on her way back to Kilgour, when suddenly, on the bend, something had sheared, the steering was gone and the car swerved into the ditch. 'If you could give me a lift to Kilgour, Mr Landon,' she said firmly, 'that would be helpful. I can phone a breakdown service from there.' Arnold announced he would be only too pleased to help.

Reluctantly, Pauline Callington got into Arnold's car and Arnold set out for Kilgour. He tried to start a casual conversation but Yates's housekeeper seemed disinclined to talk to him. She sat stiffly, unwilling to be with him, forced by circumstance to be beholden to someone she regarded as below her notice.

Arnold was pleased when they finally turned into the driveway and headed towards the house.

They had passed the stables, where Arnold intended to turn the car, since he did not want to go up to the house and possibly meet Yates, when Pauline Callington's head jerked sideways and she hissed, a sharp intake of breath.

'*Stop!*'

Arnold applied the brakes. He stared at her; she was gazing back towards the old stables, but slowly she turned her head to look at him with blank, glazing eyes.

'What's the matter?' he asked.

She was silent for a few seconds and then she began to shake. Her mouth sagged in shock. 'There's something back there, beside the stable entrance.'

Arnold hesitated, stared at her. The hairs on the back of his neck moved, prickling. 'Wait here,' he said and got out of the car.

The sturdy entrance to the old stables loomed ahead of him, warm stone in the afternoon sunshine. Beside the gateway, half-concealed in the undergrowth, was an untidy bundle. For a moment Arnold thought it was a clump of old clothing, thrown down carelessly in the grass. Then he saw the leg, and the shape of the shoe.

Patrick Yates lay on his back, staring eyes glazed against the afternoon sunlight. His arms were thrown wide, in an attitude of crucifixion. His jacket was open at the chest, as though he had held it wide, to receive the gift of death.

In the centre of his chest was the bringer of the gift, standing proud and triumphant and deadly.

CHAPTER FIVE

1

When he was finally taken to Morpeth police station Arnold was treated quite well. A chubby young constable sat with him in the canteen while he ate the haddock and chips provided. Arnold was surprisingly hungry and ate the tasteless fish quickly. His mind was blank; it was as though he did not wish to think about what he had found at Kilgour, or the hysterical way in which Pauline Callington had behaved.

The tea was hot and very sweet. He did not normally take sugar, but he drank from the mug provided by the young policeman without demur.

The room they finally took him to was small, square and barely furnished with a table and two chairs. The big man who entered a few minutes later apologized for the starkness of the accommodation, and the graffiti on one wall.

'Normally, that shouldn't happen. I mean, we rarely leave anyone in here alone. In the interview rooms a copper usually stays with you. But for some reason . . . My name's Culpeper. Detective Inspector.' He extended his hand; rather surprised by the old-worldly charm of the policeman's manner, Arnold shook hands.

Culpeper was in his mid-fifties, a large, broad-shouldered man with a comfortable face and a wistful mouth.

The crow's feet around his eyes suggested a kindliness more in keeping with helping old ladies across roads than with investigating murder incidents, though the precision of his neatly-parted, straight grey hair made Arnold feel this would be a man with a tidy mind and a tidy life, who would want his work to similarly conform.

'You've already been questioned, I know,' Culpeper said, 'and I've seen the statement you made. I thought, since I'm now taking over the investigation, it would be useful to have a chat with you, off the record, so to speak. You seem a fairly stable man, Mr Landon, not given to the kind of outbursts we've been faced with.'

Arnold's mind flickered back to the scene at Kilgour House when the police had arrived, and shuddered. Culpeper watched him carefully for several seconds; and then asked, 'Do you go along with what Mrs Callington was saying?'

'She was upset, overwrought, distraught—'

'That doesn't answer the question.'

'I . . . I haven't formed any view. I mean—'

'That was a crossbow bolt in his chest, did you know that?'

Arnold hesitated. 'I wasn't sure. I didn't touch it. I went into the house with Mrs Callington, kept her there until the police arrived.'

'And that's when she went over the top.'

Arnold nodded. It had been a curious response to the situation odd in the sense that until the police arrived Pauling Callington had been completely in control of herself. Arnold had still been looking down at the corpse of Patrick Yates when the housekeeper had walked up to join him. She had stood there, stared, and then in a controlled, calm manner, she had suggested they had better call the police. Once the phone call had been made they had sat facing each other in the library. Pauline Callington had been on the edge of her chair, hands in her lap, fingers laced, staring woodenly at the floor. No emotion had touched her; she had declined his suggestion of a drink. It was as though she was stunned or allowing her mind to wander over the past. Or perhaps she had been gearing herself up to something.

'Did it seem a contrived reaction to you?' Culpeper asked softly.

Contrived. Arnold did not know. She had changed so radically once the police arrived. Her calmness had been shattered. He could not now decide whether there had been elements of the theatre in her collapse into hysteria; he did not know the woman, did not understand her psychological make-up, knew little about her relationship with the murdered man, so could not know why she had changed from an icy silence to a raging, threatening, accusatory passion.

Culpeper was watching him thoughtfully. 'Well?' he prompted.

'I . . . I really don't know.'

'But the allegations she made about this man Enwright, do you think they have any basis in fact?'

'She was hysterical, the pressure . . .'

Culpeper's eyes were hooded, but his voice was tinged with sadness, the gloom of disbelief in human nature. 'She has put it all in a statement, but it's disjointed, and . . . *spiteful*. She seems convinced Enwright killed Mr Yates. He has the motive . . .'

Arnold had heard her, at Kilgour, shouting at the police officers, telling them she knew Enwright had killed her employer. Enwright had hated Patrick Yates because of the farm tenancy situation, and because of Yates's attitude on the bench.

'There was tension between them that apparently came to a head after the courtroom hearing. You observed that, I understand, Mr Landon.'

Pauline Callington's eyes were sharper than Arnold had realized.

'And then there's Enwright's personal hobbies to take into account,' Culpeper continued softly. 'All this hunting gear, and the prowling in the woods, his use of a bow . . .'

'But not a crossbow,' Arnold demurred.

The hooded eyelids lifted, and Culpeper stared at Arnold with brown eyes soft as an autumn hillside. 'That's right. Not a crossbow . . . There's another thing, Mr Landon. That bolt wasn't *fired*.'

'How do you mean?'

'It was thrust in by hand. A violent thrust, and maybe a calculated one, or a lucky one. It came in at an upward angle, piercing the abdomen, looks like, and slicing into lung and heart. Not a lot of power needed, oddly enough. Track of the bolt, sliding in, a child could have done it.' The eyes narrowed suddenly, watching Arnold. 'Or a woman.'

Arnold made no reply.

'Who were Mr Yates's enemies, Mr Landon, apart from this man Enwright?'

'It seems . . . it seems he was a very unpopular man,' Arnold managed.

'Would you count any females among those enemies?' An image flashed across Arnold's mind, a woman in a courtroom crying, but a woman whose grip had tensed fiercely on his arm in distress, and whose muscled shoulder could flex a bow. A woman, also, who had good reason to hate Patrick Yates.

'Suppositions . . .' he mumbled.

'Yes. But that's all we have to go on at the moment,' Culpeper said. 'Until we get hold of this man Enwright I'm not sure how far we can go, other than on general suppositions.'

'You can't find him?'

Culpeper grimaced. 'He's not at the farm. Disappeared. His father can't help us. Mrs Callington, of course, says she thinks she saw his Land Rover headed towards Kilgour when she was travelling to the village; where he's got to since, we don't know. We'll find him, of course. And if it was his vehicle going towards the house . . .'

'Mrs Callington didn't say that when I was with her.'

Culpeper regarded him owlishly. 'It's in her statement. People think they remember all sorts of things *later*, when they've had time. Remember . . . or *embroider*.' Culpeper sighed. 'Well, let's go over your own statement again, Mr Landon, and then we'll have to let you go home and take a rest, won't we?'

2

During the next few days Arnold was involved in a planning inquiry that engendered a considerable amount of heat from a group of conservationists in Northumberland. Normally, he would have followed their arguments with interest and a certain degree of sympathy, but on this occasion he found himself unable to concentrate on the matter in hand: rather, his thoughts drifted back constantly to the horror of the discovery at Kilgour. And inevitably, the interrogation by Detective Inspector Culpeper had raised so many questions in his mind that he found himself listing the enemies of Patrick Yates in his mind, over and over again.

It was not his business, but he could not tear himself away from the contemplation of it.

On the Friday evening Arnold received a call from Alan Evesham. The history professor was brusque and to the point. He wanted to know whether Arnold had turned up anything on Ailnoth.

'I'm afraid not. I've been rather busy.'

There was a short silence. 'Yes . . . getting mixed up in murder, I hear.'

'I wouldn't have put it quite like that,' Arnold demurred.

'Don't suppose you would.' Evesham paused. 'I heard something odd about the murder weapon. There's been nothing in the papers, police keeping things close to their chests, but gossip has it the murder weapon was . . . mediaeval.'

Arnold hesitated. 'It was a crossbow bolt,' he said, and waited.

There was a long silence. Something had happened to Alan Evesham's breathing. It had taken on a ragged edge.

'Well, yes, but it's none of our business, is it? Ailnoth's what we should be talking about. My time's up, just about, Landon. Agnew's called a meeting for a week tomorrow. You'll be there, I trust. Even if you haven't turned anything up, you can give me some support at least.' Evesham uttered a short barking sound. 'Agnew seems to have some respect for your . . . intuitive judgement.'

After he rang off, Arnold sat quietly in the darkening sitting room of his bungalow. His recent obsession with thoughts of the death of Patrick Yates had been upsetting; perhaps he would be able to clear his mind if he returned to the problem facing Alan Evesham. It was healthier, and saner, to look at the death of a man six centuries ago than to project again and again the visions of murder that lay in his own mind.

He decided, the following morning, to go into Morpeth and visit the central library there. It was not as extensive as the City Library in Newcastle but it had a sound local history section, and quite a good collection on building history. There was still something that niggled at him about the chapel at Langton, but he needed to read, to browse, until perhaps the thought would clarity into something positive.

He found a seat in the reference library and sought out the books he needed. He sat down and was soon lost in the detail of mediaeval building.

A century later the office of royal mason was filled by Henry Yevele. By 1356 he was sufficiently well established to be one

of the masons concerned in drawing up the regulations for the
masons' craft in London, and in 1365 he was master of the
masons, controlling (ordinant) their work . . .

After a while, somewhat impatiently, Arnold set the volume aside. It was all very well reading in Arundel's *History of Building* but there were too many sidetracks, too much emphasis upon the lives of eminent builders in those early centuries, and not enough on the practical realities of wood and stone. For something told him it was there that he might find the answer that eluded him. He pushed Arundel aside, and directed his attention to the other volumes he had selected. He finally settled with Champney's monumental work, all sixteen hundred pages of it.

He delved into the history of brickmaking. Much of it was familiar. Men had made bricks, he knew, for six thousand years. Bricks were habitually found in the neighbourhood of flourishing Roman towns such as St Albans, the old Verulamium, and Colchester, or Camulodunum as the Romans had called it. But when the Romans left brickmaking ceased and did not flourish again for almost a millennium.

Arnold leaned back in his seat, thinking for a while, and then with a quickening pulse he turned to the back of the volume and began to check the index. It was several minutes before he found the section he wanted. He turned back to the main book text.

The first evidence of a brickmaking industry occurs in
the early fourteenth century in Yorkshire, near Hull and
Beverley. The trade of the port of Hull was principally
with the Netherlands and the Baltic, where brickmaking
flourished. The church of Holy Trinity at Hull provides a
fine example of fourteenth-century brickwork. On the north
side of the chancel the early brickwork stands revealed, in
part red, in part blue, laid in broad mortar patterns . . .

Red in part, and then blue . . . The problem turned slowly in Arnold's mind, teasingly, glimmering with a half-seen light, beyond reach but there, positively and certainly. He read on, quickly, but the glow of excitement faded, as he realized he had missed the point he was looking for, the elusive, half-remembered reality. Excitement gave way to frustration and he gnawed at his lip. It was in this mood that he realized someone was speaking to him and he looked up from the book snappishly.

'What did you say?'

'I said good morning,' Tom Malling said uneasily. Arnold cleared his throat. 'I'm sorry. I was . . . involved with this book, I wasn't aware . . .'

'I'm sorry, also, to disturb you,' Malling said. 'It's just that the librarian told me the book I wanted to consult was already being used, and that you had it over here. I came across, saw it was you, and wondered whether . . .'

'Book? Which book are you talking about?' Arnold asked, confused.

'Arundel.'

History of Building? I didn't know you were interested in mediaeval building.'

Malling shifted uneasily, shuffling his feet. 'I can't say I am. It's just that some things you said, when we talked . . . And I understand there are some things in the book . . .' He half turned away, awkwardly, and Arnold stood up. 'Please, I'm sorry. I'm not using the book and it's most rude of me. Please take it.'

He handed the volume to Malling. The farmer took it almost reluctantly and then stood staring at Arnold, pale around the mouth. He held the book clutched to his chest but his mind was suddenly on other things. 'I . . . I hear it was you who . . . who found the body of . . . of . . .'

'Patrick Yates.' A slow flush coloured Arnold's uneasy cheeks. 'I'm afraid so.'

'What did he look like?'

Taken aback, Arnold thought for a moment. 'I don't understand—'

'Had he taken long to die?'

Arnold frowned and looked down at the book in front of him. He shook his head. 'I don't know. I don't think so. The impression I got from the policemen who spoke to me was that he had died fairly quickly. The shock . . .'

'I see.' Malling was silent for a while, still standing there, staring at Arnold. It took some moments before he was able to struggle out the next words. 'I understand they've now found the man they've been searching for.'

'Enwright?'

'Yes. It was on the news this morning: a man helping the police with inquiries. But local gossip has it he had gone to Aylesbury to look at a farm holding.'

'Oh yes?'

'Yates had many enemies.'

'So I understand.'

'Men . . . and women . . . You know that man Francis don't you? There's a rumour that he . . . he might be involved, rather than Enwright.'

'I wouldn't know,' Arnold said rather sharply. Malling had the capacity to startle him, make him uneasy, and more than ever Arnold was resentful of the fact that he saw something of himself in the farmer, an echo of lost days, a view of the past . . .

'There's some would say that whoever killed Yates, it would be an Act of God, an ancient retribution, a visitation of justice upon the wicked,' Malling said slowly.

Arnold raised his eyebrows. 'It was murder.'

'Do judges commit murder when they consign a man to prison for life? Does the soldier commit murder when he kills?'

'The law—'

'The law is supposed to dispense justice, but when it does not, how is justice to be obtained?' Malling shook his head and snorted angrily. 'This man Yates was a man of property but his passions and appetites were evil. He deserved to die, so there are many who will merely applaud the fact of his death.'

'Applaud an act of murder?' Arnold questioned. 'I can't believe you really accept that.'

Malling's eyes were hooded as he clutched the volume of Arundel to his chest. 'I consider we have lost sight of the realities. I'm not a religious man, and I hate freemasonry and all such chicanery, but in this modern world we have lost the capacity to seek the truth, reach it, touch it, *bring it about.* In the world of our fathers things were differently ordered; there was an acceptance of the way in which things should be done, even among the subtle craft. Perhaps it's time we looked back to those days and ordered our lives in the manner they did.'

Arnold was puzzled. 'I don't understand what you mean. The old, uncivilized times . . . we've outgrown the crudities of those periods. They can't be recalled.'

'You can say that, when you dream of stone and ancient woods?'

Nettled, uncomfortably aware that Tom Malling possessed an unwelcome insight into his emotions and needs, Arnold shook his head. 'We're talking about different things. I admire the skills of the past, and the methods—'

'But not the methods of dispensing justice?'

'The rope?'

'The justifiable killing.'

'Do you really believe it was right that Yates should die in that fashion?' Arnold demanded.

'He *deserved* to die,' Malling whispered drily.

It was suddenly more than Arnold could accept. 'Forgive me,' he said, 'I really must get on with my researches.'

Tom Malling straightened. He stared blankly at Arnold for several seconds, then nodded slowly. There was a veiled uncertainty in his eyes, as though he was puzzled by something, searching for words or actions which were now only half-understood and half-remembered. 'I'm sorry,' he mumbled. 'Thank you for . . . for the book.'

Arnold watched him covertly as he turned away and wandered towards a seat in the far corner of the room, uncertain of the direction he was taking. Arnold turned back to his own book and tried to concentrate but found it impossible to immerse himself in the text. He was annoyed: he had been working towards something, a theory about Langton and Ailnoth, but now Malling had filled his mind with images of blood again. The teasing mediaeval issue evaded him; and he could think only of Yates's body, half-hidden in the grass, sightless eyes glaring at the sky, the bolt standing upright in his chest.

When he looked up again Malling had gone. Arundel's *History of Building* was on the table. Arnold had the feeling it had not been opened, not consulted.

* * *

The newspapers carried a report the following day that a man was at Morpeth police headquarters helping them with their inquiries into the death of Patrick Yates. It did not name the individual concerned but Arnold had no doubt that it would be Nick Enwright.

When he arrived at the office he was met, inevitably, by colleagues who wanted to talk to him about it. Equally inevitably he did not want to discuss the matter. He simply wanted to forget all about Yates: the images were too clearly cut in his memory.

The Senior Planning Officer hovered at one stage, but reticence overcame curiosity and Arnold was grateful when the man went back to his office.

Hollywood Sanders was less reticent. 'It'll be him, all right. Take my word for it.'

'Who?'

'Enwright. He'll have done it. No smoke without fire. The cap fits, he'll have to wear it.'

'Are you talking about Yates's murder?'

'What else? This Enwright, he's a well-known poacher. Yates nailed the bugger on the bench. And there was this business about the tenancy he wouldn't give Enwright. The guy had all the motive in the world, and everyone knows he was a violent young sod. He'll be the one who planted that bolt in Yates. Crossbow fanatic, he is.'

'You're wrong,' Arnold suggested quietly. 'He doesn't use a crossbow, but a *longbow.*'

'Same thing, for God's sake,' Sanders said crossly. 'Crossbow, longbow — it's a bow, isn't it?'

'As I understand it, the man's been released.'

'Oh, they've let him go *for the moment.* That's the trouble with the law these days; weighted too much in favour of the guilty. Did things different in the old days, you know.' There were echoes of Malling's views. Arnold grimaced.

'Thumbscrews and racks, you mean?'

'He won't get away with it,' Sanders announced, ignoring the jibe. 'Cock-and-bull story he's got about looking around Aylesbury for a farm holding because he knew he'd never get Top Farm from Yates. Besides, some reckon that fancy woman of Yates's, Pauline Callington—'

'His *housekeeper.*'

'Don't be such an *innocent,* Arnold,' Sanders jeered. 'I was saying, this Callington piece, she reckons she *saw* Enwright's Land Rover headed for the house.'

'There are a lot of Land Rovers in Northumberland. How would she recognize Enwright's?' Arnold asked.

'I just tell you what I hear,' Sanders grumbled. 'Why are you so bloody *sceptical?*'

Possibly because Arnold found himself unable to *believe* in Pauline Callington. He did not really doubt she had been Yates's mistress at some time; nor even that she probably loved him. It was likely, or otherwise she would hardly have accepted the indignities he heaped on her in public. But he had seen her semi-hysterical and could not make up his mind whether that hysteria had been deliberate. She insisted Enwright had killed Yates . . . but perhaps her own love had turned to something else — something violent — for which Enwright could be a convenient scapegoat . . .

161

And what of the rumour that Tom Malling had mentioned? Village gossip was suggesting that Francis might have been angry enough over the verdict given in court to have taken the law into his own hands. Years in the bush could make violence second nature to a man. Arnold could guess at the lurid imaginations that would be at work.

As for Malling himself, there was something odd about him that left Arnold uneasy. He certainly had the same kind of fascination for the past that Arnold had, but there was something about Malling's interest that raised the hairs on the nape of Arnold's neck.

Or was it merely that Arnold saw in Malling too close an image of himself, the solitary, introverted loner who had only the past for company?

Grimly Arnold shook himself free from such thoughts and concentrated upon his work. He had the second inquiry to prepare for, two further files had come down from the Senior Planning Officer — and he still had not managed to capture the elusive thought that hovered at the fringes of his mind concerning Ailnoth and Langton Castle.

3

Arnold went back to Langton again at the weekend to inspect the outer walls of the ancient castle. He looked again at the ancient bricks in the building and the words drifted back to him from the account in Champney . . . *part red, part blue* . . .

But that wasn't it. There was something else, some piece of information tucked away in the recesses of his mind that he was unable to tease forth.

He went to the meeting with Agnew and Evesham still struggling to seize the information he wanted.

Professor Agnew met his courteously and offered him a cup of coffee. Alan Evesham came in a little while later. He seemed bedraggled, a line of stubble on his chin, and Arnold gained the impression the military historian had not slept well for some time. Agnew inspected his colleague critically.

'You don't look well.'

'Been marking papers,' Evesham mumbled. 'And this damned grant . . . if you'd only see your way clear . . .'

'That's the purpose of this morning's meeting,' Agnew observed urbanely. 'But you really should not take things so much to heart. The examinations you've set were not formal tests . . . they could have waited for term end. I understand it was your choice.'

'Keeping my mind off other things,' Evesham muttered, 'and keeping the minds of those young bastards on their work. Well, shall we start?'

Professor Agnew sniffed, shrugged and smiled vaguely in Arnold's direction. 'Of course. As far as I'm concerned, Professor Evesham, the support you're requesting must stand against a series of other demands made upon the research budget. I've now whittled down the submissions to a group I'm prepared to support because they seem to me to be a worthwhile series of projects which will add to our sum of knowledge. The difficulty I face over yours, as opposed to the ones I've mentioned, is that it seems to be based, essentially, upon a weak hypothesis.'

'Ailnoth—'

'The evidence you *suggest* is there is hardly of the kind that can be described as positive. If we are to back your research from our meagre funds we really must have something more concrete to go on. The Ailnoth you're interested in is hardly likely to be the *Alnith* of Langton. Unless Mr Landon is able to help us, therefore, it seems to me we've come to a dead end as far as argument is concerned.'

Evesham's lips suddenly writhed back from his teeth in a gesture of fury, perhaps brought on by tiredness, anxiety and frustration. 'Damn it, Agnew, does my project have to stand or fall on the word of an *amateur?*'

'When it has little else to stand on,' Agnew replied smoothly, 'what else is there?'

All three men were silent for a few moments. Evesham's dark, angry glance snapped across to Arnold. 'Well?' Unhappily, Arnold shook his head. 'I fear I'm unable to help.'

'What the hell's that supposed to mean?'

'It's just that—'

There was a gentle tapping on the door. It's very gentleness prevented the outburst that Evesham was preparing in order to cut across Arnold's explanation. Agnew called out, and the door was opened gingerly. A young woman stood there, one of the secretarial staff. 'I beg your pardon, Professor Agnew. There's a . . . a Mr Culpeper here.'

The big, gentle frame of the policeman eased the door open. '*Detective Inspector* Culpeper,' he said, smiling softly. 'Do you think I could have a word with Professor Evesham?'

Alan Evesham stared at the policeman with angry, red-rimmed eyes. 'We're in a meeting,' he snarled.

'It's important,' Culpeper said gently.

'So's this meeting.'

Culpeper smiled again. The smile was sad, but expectant. 'It's about a crossbow bolt.'

There was a silence in the room. The girl backed sideways, away from the door, and disappeared hastily along the corridor. Something had happened to Evesham's breathing; it had a ragged, distressed quality, an edge of panic. He stood up, tried to say something, but the words were strangled, incomprehensible.

Agnew frowned. 'Perhaps your room, Professor Evesham?'

Evesham nodded suddenly, and as Culpeper stood aside he marched out, to lead the way. Culpeper caught Arnold's glance, nodded in recognition, and walked after Evesham. Agnew stared at the floor.

Uneasily, Arnold looked about him. There seemed little point in continuing with this ill-starred meeting. He had nothing to offer these two academics anyway. It had always been a mistake: this was not his world, and he had been foolish to accept the suggestions that Agnew had made. 'I think it would be as well if I left now,' he said.

Agnew settled his troubled gaze on Arnold. 'I think so. If you have nothing to add . . .'

'I fear I just can't help. I'm sorry.'

Agnew nodded, preoccupied, and after a moment Arnold rose, shook hands with the Professor and walked out into the corridor. He walked its length, and the sunlight streamed in through the mullioned windows, casting patterns of light on the carpeted floor. At the far end of the corridor the handsome oak doors were open, leading to the stairs that would take him to the ground floor. He reached the doors, turned left, and then paused. On the wall beside him was a painting, of the Flemish school. Something stirred, in his mind, slow, turgid, the unsettling of a muddy thought.

The Flemish school. The drab figure in the tall hat stared sombrely at Arnold, the careful interior of the room picked out with precision, the stout matronly figure in the corner working at her sewing. Arnold stared at the painting, seeing it but not seeing, thinking, but with his thoughts beginning to whirl and rise and enter a confusion of acts and memories and suppositions. He closed his eyes and a red blackness descended on him as he squeezed his lids tight shut. Red . . . and black . . . *part red, part blue* . . .

Slowly, almost wonderingly, he turned and walked back along the corridor to Professor Agnew's room. The door was open. Agnew still sat dully in his chair, his brows creased with a vague, uncertain anxiety. He looked up as Arnold stood there.

'I think I can help after all,' Arnold announced.

* * *

Professor Agnew inspected his fingernails thoughtfully, observing them with a detached curiosity that suggested he had never seen them before. He chewed at his lower lip, nodding quietly to himself and then he sighed. 'Do you think you'd be able to . . . ah . . . give me chapter and verse for this?'

'I'd have to check the references, although I imagine one of your research assistants could do it as well. I think the matter is well documented.'

'Hmmm. But how did this . . . theory return to you just now?'

'I was walking in the corridor,' Arnold explained. 'I saw a painting, of the Flemish school. It was a trigger. I'd been reading in Arundel and Champney, I'd read about the brickwork at Hull, part red, part blue, and I *knew* there was something I should remember. But the painting, the *Flemish* school, it reminded me that more came from Flanders than art.'

'Bricks.'

'Precisely. It is well documented that immigrants were entering England from the Low Countries well before the end of the twelfth century. The ships that brought them, it is believed, carried bricks as ballast. They were of a notable kind, not red and blue like the Hull bricks, but red, pink and orange — and especially cream and greenish-yellow. Very large quantities of these bricks were imported, because although they first came as ballast they soon became fashionable, and much sought-after.'

'But bricks are heavy, and roads were bad—'

'So local industry emerged again. And that's the point.'

'Ailnoth?'

Arnold nodded. 'Flemish bricks were fashionable — but expensive, so they were used only in those areas where there was trade with Flanders, and easy access to sea or river. Flemish bricks are therefore concentrated in the south of England — there was a shipment in 1278 of two hundred thousand for the Tower of London alone. But you don't find them in the north of England, generally. It just wasn't an economical proposition.'

'So what happened?'

Slowly Arnold said, 'I can't be sure,' of course. It would need to be investigated. But let's put it like this, as a hypothesis. Flemish bricks were fashionable, but expensive. A local product would need to be found to satisfy the demand. Local materials were eventually found and developed, in Suffolk. Little Wenham Hall is an example there — flints, lumps of yellowish solidified mud dug from the seashore, cream and greenish-yellow bricks.'

'So?'

'We have it on record that Ailnoth worked in Suffolk, in that area.'

'That doesn't prove anything.'

'Agreed.' Arnold hesitated. 'But the point is, if you look at what has been described as the chapel outside the existing line of Langton Castle you'll see something of considerable interest. The structure is ancient. It was actually once part of the outer wall, I'm convinced. And it is based on *Roman* tiles. But then trace up the original walls and you see something else. Old bricks, not as old as the Roman bricks, but old, twelfth-century old. And *greenish-yellow in colour.*'

'Flemish bricks?'

'No. They were never brought north because of the expense. I think they're the cheaper version, Suffolk made — and brought from Suffolk by a man, a building contractor, a supplier of materials who had come north from the Suffolk area — *maybe* after he had been barred as a master mason, *maybe* to offer skilled supervision on the site, well away from the scene of his disgrace, *maybe* knowing about the Suffolk bricks because he had worked there as a master mason—'

'*Maybe* Ailnoth,' Agnew murmured.

'And *maybe* buried at Langton, along with others who died in a building accident or a sudden plague.'

Interest glittered in Agnew's eyes. Warily he said, 'You think this supports Evesham's thesis?'

Arnold shook his head. 'I don't know. It's merely a small piece of evidence that *might* be regarded as supportive of his general hypothesis that Ailnoth and Alnith are one and the same. All I'm saying—'

'All you're saying is that this might be a sufficient piece of evidence to suggest we should allow Evesham the funding to delve more deeply, investigate further.' Agnew smiled vaguely. 'Interesting . . . I get the impression that you are beginning to believe Professor Evesham's theory. He won't thank you for this, of course.'

Arnold smiled wryly and shrugged. 'I haven't really done very much, and besides—'

The door burst open violently and Alan Evesham almost tumbled into the room. His hair was standing up spikily, and his hands were shaking in anger. He glared wildly at them both as though they were indulging in some kind of conspiracy against him. '*What the hell's going on?*' he demanded.

Arnold tried to say something but·Agnew was rising to his feet. Arnold had never seen the Professor angry, but his normal urbanity was overtaken now by fury at the ill-mannered way in which Evesham had burst into his room.

'*Evesham!* How *dare* you thrust your way into my room in this way!'

'I want to know what the hell's going on,' Evesham bawled at the top of his voice. 'Someone's been into my room!'

'What on earth are you talking about?'

Evesham was almost beside himself with rage, but there was something else there in his voice which Arnold only picked up after a moment. It was panic. 'You've always said I shouldn't keep in my room what you regard as *clutter,* Agnew,' Evesham shouted hysterically. 'But no one gave you or any of your sucking-up colleagues permission to go into my room and remove items! I want to know what's happened, and I want to know who you got to do it!'

'Evesham, you'd better explain yourself,' Agnew said icily, 'and do it in a calm manner.'

There was a movement behind Evesham, and the young professor froze. Detective Inspector Culpeper stood there, looking serious but calm. 'Perhaps I should explain,' he suggested.

Evesham's eyes were red-rimmed and wild. He looked sick.

'Please,' Agnew said.

Culpeper inclined his head gravely. 'I came to see Mr Evesham about his collection of mediaeval weapons. We have been making inquiries among dealers in antiquities. The bolt that killed Mr Yates . . . there's a strong possibility that it was once in the possession of Mr Evesham.'

Alan Evesham made a gurgling sound.

'We can't be absolutely certain, of course,' Culpeper continued. 'But we can't check. It seems that the bolt Mr Evesham had has disappeared. It was stolen, he said, some time ago.'

'At the meet.' Evesham struggled out the words. 'Up at Langton—'

'And it seems that misfortunes do not visit Mr Evesham one at a time,' Culpeper observed. 'Not only the bolt seems to have been stolen—'

'Some sod's stolen the crossbow from my room as well!' Evesham declared passionately.

Culpeper caught Arnold's glance. He smiled thinly. Arnold gained the impression that the policeman did not like Alan Evesham. Nor did he believe him. The impression was strengthened when Culpeper said with a silky politeness, 'I think these are matters we can discuss further at police headquarters.'

Evesham opened his mouth to make an angry retort but stopped short as Agnew asked, 'Is that really necessary?'

Culpeper was not concerned with the reputation of the university. 'I am conducting a murder inquiry, Professor Agnew. The murder weapon was a crossbow bolt. Mr Evesham *had* one, but it mysteriously disappeared. He now tells me the crossbow itself has also disappeared. I cannot guess why this should be. But I think we can sort things out more easily if Mr Evesham comes to Morpeth to have a look at the bolt in our possession, to see if he can identify it. Then . . . then we can take a statement from him, which might help us clear up matters.'

'I thought you'd got hold of someone—'

'We have interviewed someone,' Culpeper interrupted. 'He has not been *eliminated* from our inquiries; at this stage he has not been able to help us a great deal. But we persist, and now . . .'

'I don't see how I can help,' Alan Evesham blustered.

'That remains to be seen, sir. But can we now go, so we can get it over with.'

'To Morpeth?' Evesham asked, reddening in the face.

'If you please,' Culpeper replied with a half-concealed edge of impatience in his tone.

Agnew was silent. Alan Evesham's face was white and there was an unmistakable panic in his eyes. 'This is preposterous!' he exclaimed.

'Maybe,' Culpeper replied sharply. 'Even so . . .' Evesham shot one scared, angry glance in Agnew's direction and then hurried from the room. Culpeper nodded to

Agnew and Arnold and then followed, closing the door quietly behind him.

Agnew inspected his fingernails, a slight flush staining his cheeks. Arnold sat still, unable to discard from his mind the outburst from Alan Evesham at the sherry party held by Professor Agnew. What were the words Evesham had used?

'*Extermination. Treat him like the vermin he is.*'

Startled, Arnold realized he had repeated the words aloud. Agnew was staring at him, open-mouthed. But it was not in surprise at hearing Arnold speak but rather, Arnold guessed, because the words Evesham had used on that occasion must have been heard by Agnew also, and had been in the Professor's mind now.

CHAPTER SIX

1

On the Tuesday afternoon the Senior Planning Officer called Arnold to his office. At first, Arnold thought the curiosity of the Senior Planning Officer had got the better of him. But when he was ushered into the Presence, he realized that his superior colleague was able to control such impulses. He was waved to a seat and the Senior Planning Officer turned his chair so that he was not obliged to face Arnold. Staring out of the window, he said, 'There is now a difficulty over the Kilgour application.'

'I believe so, sir, yes.'

'What do you propose to do, Mr Landon?'

'Nothing immediately, sir. The death of Mr Yates means that the application will presumably not be proceeded with, at least not until the matter of the succession is settled.'

'Did Mr Yates leave any heirs?'

'I really can't say.'

'Is there a will?'

'Once again, sir, I don't know.'

The silence that fell suggested to Arnold that he *should* know. In a disgruntled tone, the Senior Planning Officer said, 'There's been a bad press.'

'Sir?'

'Councillor Stanley, the chairman of the planning committee, has been in to see me. Council elections are due soon. He's read a piece in the *Herald* and also something in the *Journal* which declares that Yates's attitudes were bad for the estates. He's also had a few letters of the kind you already have on file. Fact is, Mr Landon, I am under a considerable degree of *political* pressure to have this planning application withdrawn.'

'I don't see how——'

'If there is no will, and if there are no heirs to the estate, what will happen to the land?' the Senior Planning Officer asked.

'It will be taken by the Crown as *bona vacantia,*' Arnold said.

'And matters will be taken out of our hands. The Crown Commissioners . . . Mr Landon, it seems to me action is necessary.'

'To do what?'

'We need to find out whether there are any heirs, or if there's a will. The local politicians want the application removed so things can simmer down. We can't really do that until we *know* there are likely to be no objections. But I'm under pressure for an early decision.'

'There's Mr Francis, of course,' Arnold suggested.

'I thought he'd fallen out of the reckoning,' the Senior Planning Officer said sharply.

'It depends,' Arnold said. 'The judgement given was that he has no right to the lands. Since they were legally owned by Patrick Yates they will go to Yates's heirs, not revert to Francis or others in Colonel Edridge's family. But that assumes the decision will stand. There is the possibility of an appeal — if Francis can afford it. And if that appeal were successful. Yates's death would become to that extent irrelevant. Francis would get the land.'

'Wouldn't that solve the problem?'

'I have a feeling,' Arnold said heavily, 'that Mr Francis could not be relied upon to behave towards the Kilgour

Estates in a manner significantly different from Mr Yates. He's not really interested in the estates as such — only in what they can give him.'

'Oh dear . . . Mr Landon?'

'Yes, sir, I understand. I'd better make inquiries.'

At least it would get him away from the suffocating gossip of the office, with its unhealthy concentration upon who might have murdered the unpopular magistrate, Patrick Yates of Kilgour.

* * *

He left Morpeth at eleven in the morning to drive into the Northumberland hills once again. He caught sight of the signpost to Ogle and wondered briefly about Alan Evesham. As far as he understood, the military historian had not been detained in police custody; he had made a statement and been allowed to leave. That he remained a prime suspect in the eyes of Detective Inspector Culpeper, Arnold did not doubt. The story Professor Evesham had told was certainly odd, though Arnold did recall a disturbance at the archery meeting at Langton. There had been a display of weapons there. Evesham had been present; an altercation had arisen and the story was that the crossbow bolt had been stolen on that occasion. It was something Culpeper would no doubt now be checking.

As for the crossbow itself, that seemed a pointless theft which had little or nothing to do with the murder of Patrick Yates, since Culpeper had intimated the bolt had been thrust into Yates rather than fired at him. Was it a piece of embroidery by Evesham? The crossbow could certainly have been stolen from his room; the notoriously untidy clutter of that room had been open to all, since Evesham had been prone to leave the door wide open.

Nick Enwright had been at the Langton meeting, and so had Wendy Gregory.

Wendy Gregory.

There were two women Arnold had to meet today, and Miss Gregory was one of them. But first, he had a call to make at Kilgour House itself.

He arrived there shortly before one o'clock. The house had a closed-in, shuttered appearance, as though it found the attention devoted to it by the press of recent days unwelcome and it had drawn in upon itself. The driveway was churned with mud: Arnold had seen several photographs in the newspapers during the last two weeks — images of the house, of Pauline Callington, face half-hidden by a raised newspaper, and of the dilapidated tenanted farms. The articles had been openly critical of the dead man's management of Kilgour, and something of the old story — Francis's side of things — had been published. It had led to the political pressure upon the Senior Planning Officer — and Arnold's visit now.

The door was answered by Pauline Callington herself.

Her face was pale, its lack of colour emphasized by the dark mourning dress she wore. Oddly, her hair was tied back with a bright red piece of chiffon, startling against the darkness of her dress. She wore no make-up and the tiny crow's feet around her eyes were more than usually noticeable, while lines of discontent around her mouth and an apparent sagging of her jawline seemed to make her look older than he had realized earlier. She was still a handsome woman, nevertheless, and still a hard one.

'What do *you* want?'

Arnold hesitated. 'Do you think I could have a word with you?'

'About what?'

'About the future of Kilgour.'

Her mouth tightened, and something moved angrily in her eyes. The anger died, to be replaced by suspicion. 'Why should that concern you?'

'The planning application.'

She frowned, considered his explanation for several seconds, then with an obvious reluctance she stepped aside, gesturing for him to enter.

Arnold followed her as she led the way to the library. Dustsheets had already been draped over the furniture, with one exception. Near the window, overlooking the meadows beyond the house, stood a handsome carved oak chair. An eighteenth-century card table stood beside it. On the table was a whisky decanter, and a half-full glass of neat whisky. Pauline Callington sat in the chair, picked up the glass and stared at Arnold challengingly. 'Well?'

He could not be certain whether the challenge related to his presence there, or to his observation of the fact she had taken to Yates's whisky bottle. Either way, she had not offered him a seat. He was not expected to stay long. He had no desire to stay long. He found her a formidable woman.

'We're concerned about the future of Kilgour, or more specifically, the matter of the planning application,' Arnold said. 'To what extent, we need to know whether it's to remain on file, or whether it will be withdrawn or proceeded with by the heirs—'

'Ha!'

Arnold hesitated, watching her nervously as she finished the whisky and poured herself another. Her colour remained pale and she seemed unaffected by the alcohol but there was a cold glitter in her eye.

'Are there any heirs? To your knowledge, I mean?'

'Yates never married,' she said snappishly. 'He was an only child. There are no known living relatives. He was alone.'

Arnold hesitated. 'Was there a will?'

'A will?' The glitter grew sharper, ice under a winter sun, and her mouth became pinched, tight in its anger and frustration. 'Oh yes, there's a bloody will — or so he said! The *bastard!* I've contacted his solicitors, I've tried the banks, I've hunted high and low . . .' She took a long pull at her whisky, then put her head back against the carved wood of the chair. Her lips writhed back mirthlessly over her teeth. 'You see a wronged woman, my friend.'

'Wronged?'

She laughed now, but still it lacked warmth or real mirth. It was self-mockery and suppressed rage that came from her, and it made Arnold nervous. 'Don't misunderstand me,' she said, 'I knew what I was getting into. I knew Yates was a hard, calculating bastard with an overlay of charm that could bring women — and men — to his bed. The men, I can't vouch for them, though I heard enough about his relationship with old Edridge, but the women, oh yes, that I *can* vouch for! He had an eye, and if his success rate dropped in recent years that was only because he couldn't be bothered any longer. He had satisfaction here, sexually, and the added pleasure of making me squirm.'

'Mrs Callington—'

'Am I making you uneasy, Mr Landon?' She laughed on a high, brittle note. 'You knew I was his housekeeper — surely you guessed what everyone else knew? Of course I was his mistress, but the reason why I stayed on here as no one else did was that we *understood* each other. He knew I was as tough — and as calculating — as he was. He respected that. And it amused him to set it all up, and then make me squirm.'

Arnold asked, in spite of himself. 'Set what up?'

'The *arrangement,* of course! I stay here, service his needs — and some of them were peculiar, believe me — and then I'd get the estates when he died. He never thought he'd live long . . . He was right about that, at least, the bastard . . .'

Arnold had thought she had loved him. He had guessed it accounted for her acceptance of public and private humiliations. Perhaps his thoughts were clear in his face for Pauline Callington stared at him contemptuously. 'It was an *arrangement.* I hated the bastard, but it was too late, I couldn't leave! He'd promised me.' Her right hand clenched suddenly in spasm and she put down her glass, her left hand trembling in passion. 'But I can't find that bloody will! He's cheated me. *Cheated* me!'

Arnold stared at her. Though the whisky had had no obvious physical effect, it had certainly loosened her tongue, for he doubted that she would have been so open with him otherwise. But the sudden thought struck him that there might yet be other secrets she would have to impart. Not to him, perhaps, but to Detective Inspector Culpeper.

'When we found Yates dead,' he said slowly, 'you were calm. But when the police arrived, you were hysterical.' She looked at him mockingly. 'Delayed shock.'

'You accused Nick Enwright of killing Yates.'

She raised her eyebrows and looked at him appraisingly. 'You've got a nerve. And you're no fool, either, are you, Landon? But there's just the two of us, so why don't we talk? Enwright? Obvious choice. The bastard wanted Yates dead-as much as I did. So why not set the police on to him? Stop him setting his gin-traps in the woods and slicing those bloody arrows into the game. And draw attention away from me, too. Why not? I didn't want to sweat away in Morpeth HQ, did I? *I needed to find that bloody will!*'

'Are you saying—'

'*Saying?*' Her words slurred suddenly, as though the alcohol finally began to take effect. 'What the hell am I saying? Nothing! I couldn't stand that bastard with his groping hands and his funny ways! All right, he was attractive at the beginning, but he hooked me in the end with cheating lies and maybe I guessed it and didn't trust him and wanted him dead, but you'll never get me to say that outside this house! And if you think you'll ever be clever enough to get me to slip up . . .' She swung her arm in a sudden, furious gesture, knocking the decanter to the floor and tipping over the card table. She stood up, staring at the whisky glass in her hand and then she threw that down too, and stood there breathing hard and furiously. The whisky in the decanter gurgled as it lapped on to the carpet, a steady stain spreading like blood on the dark red pile.

Pauline Callington raised her head and stared at Arnold, fully in control of herself again. The rage in her eyes had subsided; it was as though the last few minutes had never happened. 'I don't think there's anything more I have to say to you now, Mr Landon. Please leave.'

Arnold left. He got into his car and drove away. As he pulled past the library windows he looked up. He caught a glimpse of her face as she stood there, looking out over the hills. He had the impression that she would not be seeing him, but what she had lost. Or what she had never really possessed.

2

Thoughtfully, Arnold made his way back towards the village.

He was in a confused state of mind. The attitudes that Pauline Callington had demonstrated to him were entirely unexpected. When Arnold had found the body of Patrick Yates she had seemed controlled. Her later hysteria in face of the police had seemed to him to be a matter of delayed shock. Now he knew that the hysteria had been deliberate — it had been the presentation of an unreal reaction. Pauline Callington had wanted to show to the police a feminine shock and horror of the kind they would have expected in an innocent woman. But its real purpose had been to divert attention, away from herself.

Did that mean she had something to hide? Arnold weighed the matter in his mind. It *could* have been a genuine attempt to avoid involvement, questioning and the pressure that would inevitably have been brought in a murder inquiry.

On the other hand, it could have been something more sinister.

He went over the sequence of events. Pauline Callington claimed she had left Patrick Yates to go shopping in Langton. He was alive when she left. Her car had broken down, she had obtained a lift from Arnold and it was he — the outsider — who had found the body in the shrubbery.

But was there not another scenario that was a possibility? They had only Pauline Callington's word for the series of events. There was the possibility that she had had a violent row with Yates. She *could* have become so incensed with the discovery of his true attitude towards her that she herself had killed him, in her violent passion. She was a formidable woman, on that point Arnold was clear. And he had no doubt she could have planned — *and* perhaps executed — the events thereafter.

If she *had* killed Yates in anger, she would have been cool enough and controlled enough to drive down to the village, perhaps *arrange* the car breakdown by damaging the steering linkage, and then to wait for someone — Arnold as it happened — to come along and provide her with an alibi.

Arnold frowned. It was possible. But when did she discover about the will . . . or lack of it? Before Yates's death, or after? And the car breakdown: she had claimed it was due to a steering fault, but had it been confirmed? Had the police checked? They'd made no suggestion that it had been tampered with, but . . .

Arnold shook his head. People bothered him in a way stone and wood did not. People gave him problems of emotional upset.

Of the kind he'd have to face, surely, with Wendy Gregory.

She and Francis were living together, of course. And if Francis was at her cottage and Arnold arrived asking about the future, there'd surely be a scene of some kind. He went over the kind of approaches he could make when he arrived there.

In the event, he was relieved: there was no answer to his knock at the cottage door. He waited for a while, uncertainly, and then he made his way out through the little white-painted wooden gate, got back into his car, and with a feeling of release drove up the hill past the church to the castle above the fields.

He would have to wait, of course. There was no point in returning to the office in Morpeth. He would wait an hour or two, then go back and see if they had returned. Meanwhile, he could fill in his time by doing a last check at Langton Castle.

The afternoon was overcast but warm, and a slanting sun sent rays of light through the clouds towards Cheviot. Arnold sat for a while above the outer walls of the castle and thought about the centuries it had seen, the men who had tramped its cold walls in the height of winter, the people who had prayed in the chapel, the lovers who had used the walls as shelter during warm summer nights.

Then he went down and looked again at the line of the scarp slope, and the ancient Roman tiles at the base of the copse-hidden structures, and at the cream and greenish-yellow bricks that had come from Suffolk hundreds of years ago.

Whether he was right or wrong was unimportant, he guessed, as far as Alan Evesham was concerned. The light of considered interest in Professor Agnew's eyes had convinced Arnold that there was now enough evidence to at least give some credibility to Evesham's claims, and there would be every possibility that Agnew would release finance to support Evesham's studies in Ailnoth and the buildings of the north. Always supposing Evesham did not have other priorities to deal with — like making it clear to the police that he had had nothing to do with the murder of Patrick Yates.

Suddenly Arnold felt weary. He climbed back up to the ridge and took the seat he had taken when he first looked down into the copse. The sun was warm on his face as he put his head back and closed his eyes. His thoughts began to drift. He remembered the sight of a sheepdog, racing across a field to greet its master, and the warmth of old stone under the summer sun. He lost his sense of the present and remembered the Old Wheat Barn, unused for centuries but still retaining the marks of a genius, the ancient joints built by John of Wetherby. Then there was that bridge of mist he had crossed to go to an old manor house where the secrets of centuries had lain hidden behind stone cellar walls, a passageway to the past. His thoughts were confused, blurring images of yesterday and last year, as the vagueness of sleep drifted over him and he dozed in the sunshine, dreaming of death, and his father, and the warm tints of coloured tiles in a wall.

He woke with a start. He stretched, then stared at his watch in disbelief.

It was almost 5.15.

He rose. His limbs were stiff. He looked about him for a few minutes, then reluctantly made his way back down to his car. He drove down to the village.

When he pulled up outside the cottage it still looked deserted. He opened the gate and entered the small front garden. He knocked at the door: the house echoed hollowly, as though it had been long since emptied and abandoned. Arnold was not certain whether he should wait any longer. He had not eaten since breakfast that morning and now his stomach was beginning to complain.

The best plan would be to go to the local pub in the village and get something to eat and drink. Pubs also dispensed information, if you were lucky.

The public house was called the Red Lion. The sign above the door stated that the licensee was one Sid Wright.

It was Mrs Wright who was serving behind the bar. She was a lean, pinched woman with a sharp nose and sharper eye. There was something about her mouth that suggested she disapproved of Arnold, and she certainly did not strike him as the chatty type so he retired with his drink, and the menu, to a corner of the room.

In a little while the lady of the house vanished into the back and the landlord himself stood behind the bar. He seemed to be of more promising material. He was large, a tubular sixteen stone, and sported a pair of walrus whiskers that dragged attention away from the shiny nakedness of his skull. He wore a blue shirt and yellow sweater, and he was sweating. Dark stains appeared in the faded yellow of his armpits. Arnold wondered whether he'd been having a hard time in the back with his wife: working now in the bar he'd be likely to lose a few litres in perspiration.

Arnold went up and ordered a half of lager. He asked Sid Wright if he'd like a drink. The answer was a pint. It almost vanished at the first swallow.

Sid Wright cocked an inquisitive eye in his direction. 'Stranger around here?'

'More or less.'

'Passing through? Or press?'

'Neither, really. On business.'

'What kind is that?'

Arnold hesitated. 'I've just called in at Wendy Gregory's cottage.'

'Oh aye.' Sid Wright leered. '*That* kind of business.'

'I was looking for Bob Francis.'

'He wor living there for a while, for sure.'

'*Was* living there?'

'Right. Moved out, few days since, now.' The tubular landlord leaned forward confidentially, elbows on the bar, and winked at Arnold with a conspiratorial left eye. 'Way of the world, if you know what I mean.'

'I don't understand.'

'Ah, you know how it is. Didn't you hear the story? Living up yonder he was, with his wife, but started this thing going with Miss Gregory. PE teacher, you know — 'andsome enough lass. His wife found out and threw him out. So he came to live with Wendy Gregory. A few scenes in the village, Miss Gregory and Mrs Francis, but Bob Francis, well, he came out of it well enough. Talk is, he used some of Miss Gregory's money to support his claim for the Kilgour Estates in the courts. Funny business, hey?'

'Funny?'

'Manner of speaking. I mean, his wife throws him out, he shacks up with Miss Gregory, he loses his claim against Yates and then our friend and magistrate gets killed. Days later, things go sour between Miss Gregory and Francis, and he walks out after a big row. *Talk* is, it's because she reckons he was only interested in her while she could help him, and since she can't raise cash for an appeal, he'll be moving on.'

So perhaps his visit to see Francis and Miss Gregory would no longer be necessary, Arnold thought. Francis could not afford an appeal — Wendy Gregory had no more money to give him and they had, in any case, split up. Cheerfully, he asked what Mr Wright had on the menu.

'Homemade soup, Cumberland sausage.'

It sounded good, and Arnold discovered half an hour later that it was good. He dallied over the meal and, since he had nothing pressing back at home, washed it down with two glasses of lager. A few people, obviously regulars, drifted in and a young couple sat for a while, waiting for it to get dark before slipping out for an evening walk.

At length the landlord came over to clear away Arnold's plates. 'Police were round this morning, you know.'

'Police?'

'They were looking for Bob Francis. I just been talking to Fred Singer, you know? He reckons he spoke to them this morning. They was making inquiries about this Francis feller. Fred, he says it's in connection with the murder of Patrick Yates.'

'I see.'

'They was back, late this afternoon. They asked Wendy Gregory about him, because seems like they can't get hold of Francis. He's skipped, like. Fred and Tom Malling was in the village when they left and Fred reckons she came out of her cottage very red in the face. I can guess what they said to her! I mean, the bloke she'd shacked up with, suspected of murder!'

'They're still looking for Francis?'

'Guess so.' Mr Wright stroked his expansive belly and considered the matter. 'My guess also is they won't be long making an arrest. I mean, where can be run to, like? Bad business, but not for trade. When the press came in like hordes last week we did quite well. A trial now, and that'd keep us through the winter.'

'What about Wendy Gregory?'

'Fred reckons she shot off in that red car of hers. Him and Tom had to move quick to get out of the way when she went around the corner.'

'Do you think she's gone to warn Francis, or to find him?'

The landlord shrugged, lifting his rotund frame with an effort. 'Shouldn't think so. Fred was saying she went off in the direction of Hampton. She's got an old mother there, about twenty miles off. Goes over regular, like. She'll have gone for a shoulder to cry on, but gossip in the village is she'll get no more than she deserves, comin' between man and wife. The old lady, her mother, she's a hard nut, I'm told, and she won't offer Miss Gregory much by way of sympathy. I reckon the parent-teacher association at the Broadwood school won't be none too pleased either. I think Miss Gregory will get a rough ride there, too. As for Francis — my bet is he's runnin' for cover. And back trackin' like the fox he is, to hide his trail.'

It all seemed too remote now, for Arnold. He sipped his third lager and thought of Nick Enwright with his long-bow and gin-traps, hunting at night, Alan Evesham with his crossbow and passion for mediaeval weapons; Tom Malling expressing his dislike for the freemasons on the hill above Langton; Wendy Gregory, the third side of a triangle involving an errant husband and a bitter wife. And Bob Francis, possibly on the run from the police after wreaking his revenge on the man who had denied him what he regarded as his rightful inheritance. But Arnold need have no more to do with these people than he did with the embittered, frustrated woman who still searched the crannies of Kilgour House.

He finished his lager and ordered another, remembering again the man who had lain with his face upturned to the sky with the bolt planted solidly in his chest.

* * *

It was dusk before Arnold finally left the Red Lion. He sat in his car for several minutes, warm, generally content, and at peace with the thought that further action on his part with regard to the Kilgour Estates would be unnecessary. He started the car, let in the clutch and drove away from the village.

He hesitated at the crossroads, wondering whether to take the short cut home across the hills to the A1. He decided against it. The winding back roads were more pleasant. He had plenty of time. He was in a comfortable frame of mind.

Just four miles later, as his headlights picked out the red car abandoned at the roadside, his peace of mind was shattered. He slowed, then stopped. He got out of the car. It had been returning towards Langton, this vehicle half in the ditch. It was empty, but the windscreen had been shattered.

Arnold went back to his car and collected his torch. In the dim evening light he flicked it on and shone it into the car. On the passenger seat was a short piece of old iron. It had been forged into the semblance of a crossbow bolt.

3

The car was lying with its nearside wheels in the ditch some forty yards from a bend. Beyond the car the hill rose: a straggling hedge led upwards to a swathe of trees lifting to the skyline, birch and alder and horn beam. The incident must have happened shortly before Arnold had reached the spot: he could still hear the ticking noise of the cooling engine.

Irresolutely, Arnold stood with his torch swinging about across the field, the narrow beam losing its power as it lanced against the hill. Dusk had now changed to darkness as heavy clouds built up from the west, and Arnold felt he detected rain in the air as he raised his head and sniffed at the wind. He flashed his torch upwards to the trees, and thought he heard a swift thrashing sound. He paused, and next moment his worst fears were confirmed as he heard a cry.

It was the voice of a woman, high, scared and panic-stricken. Almost without thinking, Arnold scrambled over the narrow hedge and began to run up towards the darkening trees.

His action was instinctive, and the blood pounded in his veins as he ran. The slope of the hill quickly made his legs ache, and he slowed as he neared the band of trees that led to the brow of the hill.

He stopped, breathing hard, and after a few moments raised his torch to send a slow sweep of light across the darkness of the trees. The leaves glittered back at him, he thought he caught the glint of an animal's eyes in the undergrowth, and irresolutely he moved forward, carefully, his heart pounding in his chest from the exertion of his run up the hill and the tension that affected him.

A rustling noise to his right made him swing around quickly: something scuttled through the undergrowth, disturbed by his approach. The hairs prickled on the back of his neck and his skin was abnormally sensitive, almost aching, as he swung the torch again.

'*Please . . . !*'

The call was desperate and cut off: he could not see the woman but he had caught the general direction and he ran forward, thrashing his way into the woods almost unthinkingly, not knowing why she hid among the trees, and not understanding the nature of the terror that affected her.

Twenty yards into the trees he stopped, and the silence of the wood swept around him like a suffocating blanket, with sky shut out under the canopy and a darkening moon losing its faded brilliance. He flashed the torch ahead of him in a long, slow sweep.

Then he saw her.

It was the whiteness of a nervous hand, half-raised, a signal against the darkness of the trees. She was kneeling or crouching down. He could not see her face, merely the gesturing hand, and he hurried forward, thrashing his way through nettles and scrub, the light dancing crazily in front of him until he reached the denser undergrowth where she was half hidden.

'What—'

'*For God's sake!*'

The woman grabbed at him, dragging him off balance, and with her free hand she struck at the flashlight, dashing it from his hand. He fell to one knee, pulled down by the urgency of her grip, and his knee burned as a thorn drilled its way into his kneecap.

'What on earth are you doing?' he demanded, groping for the flashlight. He picked it up, and for a quick moment the light played on the woman's face before she again grabbed at it, tearing it from his grasp.

It was Wendy Gregory, wild-eyed, hair in disarray, mouth open and panting and scared. The light flicked out. '*Do you want us killed*?' she hissed in terror.

She was lying on one hip, her back against the bole of a tree, glaring up at him in the darkness. He shook his head in puzzlement. 'What the hell's going on?'

'He's out there, with a bow!'

'A bow?' Arnold repeated stupidly.

'Enwright, for God's sake! He's trying to kill me! He's fixed things so that Bob is suspected for the murder of Yates, but he knows I'll never rest until I clear Bob, and so he waited for me in the roadway, until I returned from my mother's, and then he launched that crossbow bolt against me, smashed the car window—'

'But you can't be serious!'

'Serious, hell!' Wendy Gregory snarled. 'What do you think I'm lying here for? The car went into the ditch and I scrambled out. I saw him at the side of the roadway: he had the crossbow. At first, I could just make him out like a dark shadow, then I saw him raise the bow . . . I ran, just ran for cover, up the hill to these trees, but I heard him come after me, blundering about in the darkness and I lay low, then I saw your lights and when you stopped I called out . . . But for God's sake keep *down*! He knows where I am now, thanks to your lighting his way to us. We must keep quiet, keep down, and then we'll have to run for it!'

She was panic-stricken, almost incoherent, but there was something wrong, something that lurched incomprehensibly in Arnold's mind as she gasped out her terror. He could not see her face, but her grip was still fierce, strong and hard as it had been that day in the courtroom when a different kind of emotion had held her.

Arnold reached for the flashlight, took it from her. He hesitated, then depressed the switch. Nothing happened: the contact must have been damaged, or the bulb broken. Wendy Gregory's breath was harsh, painful in the silence of the woods. Arnold waited, and listened.

Someone was moving awkwardly through the trees some thirty yards away. Even as he realized it he heard a snapping sound, a metallic click and something came whirring noisily towards them, carving its deadly way through the scrub, until it clattered heavily against the tree behind them.

Suddenly, Arnold was convinced.

'Come on!' he shouted, grabbed Wendy Gregory by the elbow, and pulled her to her feet. They stood upright, and she was shaking violently. For a moment Arnold did not know which way to go, but realizing the trees still gave them protection of a kind they would lack in the open field, he plunged forward, away from the noise to their left, deeper into the trees, ascending the hill as the hunter behind them struggled to notch a fresh bolt into the mediaeval weapon he held.

Low branches whipped at them as though trying to slow them, bar their progress, but Arnold, head down, half dragged the crying woman through the scrub and undergrowth, deep into the bank of bracken that loomed up ahead of them below the brow of the hill. The going became steeper, and the bracken thicker so they were struggling, breath rasping in their chests as they toiled up to the ridge. There was a shout from behind them, fifty yards back, maybe further, compounded of rage and passion and then something whirred at them again, but across to their right, out of range and in the wrong line. Arnold glanced back and thought he saw movement, a man scrambling through the trees below them, but he could have been mistaken.

An iron band seemed to have clamped across Arnold's chest and he stopped, deep in the bracken, his legs almost giving up. Wendy Gregory pressed hard behind him, nearly causing him to fall. Her teeth were chattering and she pushed against him, younger, fitter, terrified. Arnold struggled on, clawing his way forward through the ferns and ahead of them the trees thinned on the brow of the hill a dark skyline emerging, heavy with cloud, edged with pale moonlight.

The girl slipped, feet sliding in the earth below the ferns, and as she fell Arnold lost balance also, tumbling down, face scratched by stiff dead bracken. He shouted at her in spite of the tearing pain in his chest, dragged her to her feet and they lurched forward again, seeking the skyline, wanting the screen of the hilltop so they could run on, down in the darkness towards the haven of the distant village.

It was then that the scream cut across their panic.

It was a scream of pure agony. It pulsed against the hill, echoing through the trees, and it shocked them, brought them to a halt. It came again, like an animal in torment, and there was a thrashing, furious sound, a thudding noise and then a long wailing note, a human being in pain, the drawn-out tearing note of a man in excruciating agony.

Arnold could see the pale shape of Wendy Gregory's face — her mouth dark and open as it gasped for breath, the eyes shadowed sockets of fear — and he slipped his hand under his jacket, feeling for the thudding of his heart, heaving to catch his breath.

The wailing died, subsiding to a series of short, moaning cries. Then the silence came back as it had been earlier, and the hill waited.

When the slow, shuffling, dragging sound came to them, Arnold turned his back and dragged Wendy Gregory over the hill top.

The lights of the village twinkled, some three or four miles across the fields. Below them, to their right, the road swung pale under the fading light. Arnold hesitated. The woman was still shaking, her hand tightly grasping his, and she was still riven by panic. Gently, Arnold said, 'I think we're all right now.'

'Please, no, we must . . .'

'No, wait.'

They stood, and the trees behind them were quiet. A light breeze rose, ruffling Arnold's damp hair, and gradually his breathing slowed, the thunder in his chest subsiding. Wendy Gregory's own urgency began to ease. She leaned against him and he half-supported her as she began to cry, racking sobs that tore at her but oddly calmed her, for in a little while she stopped trembling and stood away from him.

'What happened?'

Arnold could not be sure, but he could guess. He stood there in the darkness of the hill and he thought about her panicked words earlier, and the scream among the trees. He thought of Alan Evesham and his cluttered room, and a dog streaking wildly across a field. He remembered the harsh proud iron in Patrick Yates's chest and what Yates and Bob Francis had had in common. And he thought of Ailnoth and times past and the men of subtle craft.

'I think it's all right, now, Miss Gregory,' he said. 'We can cut down to the road and make our way back to my car.'

She was reluctant, but eventually trusting. She walked close to him as they descended the hill.

Halfway down, they heard the coughing roar of an engine coming to life and the lights of a vehicle lit up the road, lurching off a sidetrack to make its way back towards Langton.

'Yes,' Arnold said sadly. 'We're all right now.'

4

The Land Rover stood in the yard, its door open. Arnold stood beside the door: the courtesy light was on and on the floor of the vehicle, below the driving seat, he could see the dark patch. He touched it: it was sticky. He wiped the blood from his fingers on the side of the vehicle, then turned and went up to the house.

The door at the main entrance was slightly ajar. He entered the silent house, moving carefully and quietly. The light groaning sound finally drew him to the sitting room.

The man he was looking for lay stretched out in the sitting-room chair, his leg raised and resting on a pouffe. An attempt had been made to stop the flow of blood: a piece of wood had been twisted inside a strip of cloth to form a rough tourniquet. The attempt had not been successful: the cloth was badly stained, there was a pool of blood on the floor and spreading across the pouffe, and the man himself was ashen in colour, his eyelids flickering weakly as he watched Arnold come in. He opened his mouth to speak but Arnold ignored him, walking past him to pick up the phone and dial the emergency services for an ambulance.

Arnold had taken Wendy Gregory in the car to the Red Lion. While she had been attended to for shock and he had taken a stiff drink to calm his own nerves, the police had been called. Arnold had sat alone with his whisky, deep in thought. When he had finished the drink and had regained control of himself he had left Miss Gregory in the publican's care and driven away from the village.

The man's eyes watched him for a little while as he sat down, waiting for the ambulance. At last the words struggled out. 'How did you know?'

'That it was you?' Arnold shrugged sadly. 'I didn't know, but I guessed. Miss Gregory . . . she thought it was Nick Enwright out there in the woods. But she talked of seeing you merely as a dark shadow, and she spoke of you blundering your way through the trees. Nick Enwright was an experienced hunter, used to working at night. He wouldn't have blundered about: he'd have moved silently and quickly. And then there's the clumsy business about the crossbow . . . Enwright would never have used such an old, inaccurate weapon. Not when he had an efficient method of destruction in his longbow.'

Arnold was silent for a while, watching the man. He tightened the tourniquet and the eyes flickered again. 'I feel nothing, It's numb.'

Arnold nodded. 'The ambulance will be here soon.'

'It would have been better to leave me, alone.'

Arnold understood. 'I couldn't do that. I thought things through, guessed it could possibly be you, and realized that where Enwright wouldn't have blundered into one of his own traps, you could have done.'

The man in the chair nodded sleepily. 'A gin-trap . . . it almost sliced through my leg.'

'I realized when you drove your Land Rover away from where you'd had it parked that you'd be likely to go home. I couldn't just leave you to die . . . You see, I always felt we had some things in common, and in some ways thought alike. But I never really attached much to your statement that you thought Yates deserved to die. Then I wondered what Yates and Bob Francis and Wendy Gregory had in common, and

I half-realized what would have been in your mind. It was Richard atte Chirche who was the key.'

'Richard atte Chirche . . .' The man's tone was drowsy. 'They ordered things so much better . . . justice . . .'

'But why now?' Arnold asked quietly. 'Why did you kill Yates after all these years?'

The man squirmed uncomfortably in the chair and moistened his dry lips. 'Years . . . so long ago . . . But for me it's never changed. I hated him. He used my wife, took her away from me, and then coldly discarded her. I loved her, it wouldn't have mattered, but she killed herself when she knew he didn't want her, and she realized how she had betrayed me. She was always here, you know, all the years after she died, she was still with me. I thought of her each day and waited for justice to catch up with Patrick Yates. But it never did, and one day I talked with you on the hill—'

'It couldn't have been I who made you—'

'No. But you made me think of the past, and how it can be as real — more real — than the present. And I talked with you of the sworn masons and Richard atte Chirche and I knew that justice would never come, that I had to take it into my own hands . . .'

'You stole the bolt from Evesham's collection at Long Meadow, the day of the archery meeting.'

Tom Malling sighed. 'It was on the spur of the moment. Perhaps I had blood on my mind then, but I can't remember . . . it was there, old, mediaeval, an instrument of death. No one saw me, I just walked away . . .'

'And the crossbow?'

'That was later, the day we were at the university together. I walked past his room, saw the crossbow and I just walked in, dropped the weapon through the open window and collected it from the grass a few minutes later.' A wry smile touched his pained mouth. 'Though if I'd walked out past the porter with it, I don't think he'd have noticed.'

'But you didn't use the bow when you killed Yates.'

Malling's eyes were glazed. He thought for a while, silent, then he shook his head gently. 'I couldn't get the damn thing to work. But I was obsessed with it, using it as a sworn mason might have. But in the end, when I drove to Kilgour, he looked so surprised. The bolt . . . it went in so easily and all I could think of was of the ancient days, the men of subtle craft . . .'

Both men were silent for a while as Arnold observed the glitter of excitement in Tom Malling's eyes. When the light died again he said, 'I still don't understand why you tried to kill Wendy Gregory.'

'The bow,' Malling muttered. 'I worked on it, fashioned some bolts that would suit. I used it, in the fields . . .'

'What about Wendy Gregory?' Arnold persisted.

Malling stared at him for several seconds, uncomprehending. 'The woman . . . you don't understand . . . But she was no different no better than Yates, in her own way! All those years ago Yates took my wife from me, treated her so badly that she put her head in a gas oven. He had to pay for that. But how was Wendy Gregory different? I stood in the street when the police came to her cottage, looking for that fool Francis. I saw her come out, angry and upset because her lover had walked out on her. But what of the marriage she had destroyed? What of the woman — the wife — Francis had left, for her? She broke that marriage as Yates broke mine, and she was no different from Yates, and I knew she had to die ruining Mrs Francis's life . . .'

Hardly that, Arnold thought, as he remembered the hard, spiteful woman he had met at Station Cottage when he had first sought out Bob Francis. For Malling she had been the innocent partner in a game of seduction, a wronged wife with an errant husband. As he had been a wronged husband, with an errant wife.

'She came out, took her bright red car to go to her mother's. I saw her go; she almost ran us down. I had plenty of time. I went back to the farm. I got the crossbow and I drove along till I came to the sidetrack. I waited. It was easy. When I saw her coming, in the dusk, I ran down to the road and I fired the bolt, smashed her windscreen. She ran for the trees . . .'

'Where's the weapon now?' Arnold asked quietly.

Malling shook his head. 'When I stepped on the gin-trap I dropped it, lost it. I had to . . . to tear myself free . . . the pain, and the blood . . . But I got back to the Land Rover, and my leg was numb then . . .'

He had driven back the couple of miles, his blood soaking the floor of the Land Rover. His attempt to murder Wendy Gregory had been clumsy: with the ancient weapon and the handmade bolts Malling had never really stood much chance of hitting her among the trees, in the darkness.

Arnold recalled how the bolts had flown wild in the darkness, wide of the target. It had been an ill-conceived, badly prepared attempt to commit again a crime that itself had been badly planned, though lucky in its successful execution.

Arnold had been up at Langton hill that day when Patrick Yates had died. He had seen Malling's sheepdog racing back across the fields to greet its returning master. Arnold had seen the dog, but not the Land Rover driving back to the farm. He could not have known that Malling was returning from murder, and yet the image of that dog had remained with him. He shuddered. Had his mind touched Malling's then, too?

'I'm tired,' Tom Malling said, and closed his eyes. Outside, Arnold heard the clangour of the ambulance's warning siren.

* * *

It was several days before Arnold found time to go to the library, to seek out Arundel again. He had had to make a series of statements before Detective Inspector Culpeper. He had had to explain himself to an anxious Senior Planning Officer. His immediate superior had been concerned to discover whether the planning problems really were over. Arnold considered they were. It seemed Pauline Callington had not found the will she sought and the chances of Bob Francis raising money seemed slim. He had turned up again, having gone to ground in Teesside. Arnold suggested his cause was now a lost one and the Kilgour Estates would probably go to the Crown as *bona vacantia*.

Whether that would mean Nick Enwright would get his tenancy of Top Farm was questionable: there was a rumour that he was entering an agreement down south anyway, in the Aylesbury area. The other tenants of Kilgour were relatively happy, however: Arnold guessed they would be hopeful of receiving better treatment under the Crown Estates than they had under the regime of Patrick Yates.

'Not that it is any of our business,' the Senior Planning Officer suggested.

'No, sir,' Arnold agreed.

But Detective Inspector Culpeper was still puzzled. It showed in his glance when he questioned Arnold, and when he read over Arnold's statement. He could understand Arnold's part in the events, but he was still unable to grasp the reality of Tom Malling's motivation. Revenge, yes, for the suicide of his wife, and a long, brooding resentment that finally banked up into a fire that killed Patrick Yates. But the pursuit of Wendy Gregory was another matter. 'He must be crazy,' he suggested.

It was a point of view. Arnold tried to explain about the past, about the way it could sometimes bear more reality than the present. He tried to tell Culpeper that there were days when he himself, high on a windy crag, could smell the heather the way the Romans had, and see a hawk soar as hawks had soared for a thousand years. On the fells of the border country there were ancient tracks, and on a frosty night, in the moonlit valleys, you could hear owls hoot the way they had called for centuries.

Culpeper could not understand how the past had become real for Tom Malling, real in all its crude solutions to a problem.

In the library, Arnold finally found the passage he had read long ago, and the passage Malling had wanted to re-read, that day he had spoken to Arnold in the library.

William Twyford and Richard atte Chirche with another mason were designated as official building inspectors in 1375. They were sworn to report nuisances and encroachments, to divide property, to issue bye-laws relating to party walls, and stillicides. In 1376 Richard atte Chirche was appointed 'sworn mason'. In this capacity he was given a status that can be described not only as judicial but also as executive, carrying out the sentences determined upon. The 'sworn masons' had become by this time adjudicators not merely of boundary and tenement disputes but as 'sercheours of wronges' and adjusters of the morals of the communities in which they held sway. As members of the gild they forced the following of ordinances; as men of the subtle craft they adjudicated upon craft disputes; but as 'sworn masons' they took upon themselves the powers of life and death, in a society where the law was uncertain, the King's justice distant, and the need for justice urgent and demanding. There is some evidence that executions actually took place, in cases of theft and adultery within the gild. Few cases were recorded by way of documentation; the sworn masons remained an esoteric branch of a secret gild, which died out in the fifteenth century . . .

Tom Malling had hated the masons but had drawn the distinction between the seventeenth-century shadow and the reality of the fourteenth-century need. His misunderstanding of that time, and its relationship to the present, had cost Patrick Yates his life.

He had not been a man of the subtle craft but he had taken on the cloak of the sworn mason. And in the end he had been unable to distinguish between the righting of wrongs, and murder.

THE END

ALSO BY ROY LEWIS

Thank you for reading this book.

If you enjoyed it please leave feedback on Amazon or Goodreads, and if there is anything we missed or you have a question about, then please get in touch. We appreciate you choosing our book.

Founded in 2014 in Shoreditch, London, we at Joffe Books pride ourselves on our history of innovative publishing. We were thrilled to be shortlisted for Independent Publisher of the Year at the British Book Awards.

www.joffebooks.com

We're very grateful to eagle-eyed readers who take the time to contact us. Please send any errors you find to corrections@joffebooks.com. We'll get them fixed ASAP.